THE LINKMAN

Rick Telly awakens to find his hired man dead and his four horses missing. He is forced to track the killer on foot, which leads him to an emigrant wagon train. The situation calls for caution, until he is befriended by Betts Calhoun, the wagon-master's daughter, and becomes involved in defending the wagon train from ambush by a band of renegades. Betts Calhoun is taken captive, and Telly becomes a manhunter.

CHARLES BURNHAM

THE LINKMAN

Complete and Unabridged

LINFORD
Leicester

First published in Great Britain in 1993 by
Robert Hale Limited,
London

First Linford Edition
published July 1995
by arrangement with
Robert Hale Limited,
London

British Library CIP Data

Burnham, Charles
The Linkman.—Large print ed.—
Linford western library
I. Title II. Series
813.54 [F]

ISBN 0–7089–7748–0

Published by
F. A. Thorpe (Publishing) Ltd.
Anstey, Leicestershire

Set by Words & Graphics Ltd.
Anstey, Leicestershire
Printed and bound in Great Britain by
T. J. Press (Padstow) Ltd., Padstow, Cornwall

This book is printed on acid-free paper

1

Horse Tracks

THE old soldier sat on a stump trickling coal oil along the sawtooth-edge of his ten-foot crosscut saw. Nearby, also in tree shadows, the younger man was canting a small rat-tail file putting an edge back where an embedded stone had dulled his limbing axe.

The sun was high, every variety of obnoxious flying insect, some of which bit, circulated amid shafts of penetrating sunlight and forest shadows.

Except mosquitoes; there was no still water within ten miles of their cutting ground on Oat Mountain.

The older man was grey, grizzled and lined. He was also taciturn. All the younger man, whose name was Richard Telly, knew of the old soldier was that he had been wounded during the war, twice with musket balls, once by a bayonet.

His name was Gabriel, he had been raised in the border state of Missouri. His father had also been Gabriel; he had perished at Harper's Ferry with old John Brown, cornered like a rat with others when Union officer, Captain Robert E. Lee, had given them a choice. They had fought to the death — except for John Brown. He was hanged from a peach tree.

Richard Telly had hired the old soldier three years back. Telly had a two-man cow ranch down in the grassland country. Ever since the old soldier had been with Rick Telly, they had stripped a wagon to its running gear, driven into the late summer forested uplands of Oat Mountain and 'made' winter wood.

It was hard work, but since neither the older man nor the younger one felt impelled to hasten, they worked only until the equipment required care, then loafed a little before returning to the downed logs.

Rick Telly did not drink but Gabriel always had a croaker-sack-wrapped jug on these trips from which he drank now and then. It was, he had once told Rick, the only way he knew to keep an old, tiring body going all day without aches and pains slowing a man down.

Today it was hot; a vast canopy of treetops filtered direct sunlight but the heat, slow-building all morning, made sweat run like water by afternoon, which was when they'd quit for the day.

Their camp was beside a creek with water as clear as glass. It usually required about four, sometimes five days to down enough big firs, chase them onto the running gear and head back down to the ranch.

They had four horses to pull the rig up there, and to lean into their britchings going back down.

Four fourteen-hundred-pound horses

had little trouble pulling the stripped down old wagon up to the timber, but if they had weighed twice as much they could not have held it back on the downhill route when it was loaded.

For that chore Rick and Gabriel blocked the rear wheels with a logging chain wound through and fastened to a big green sapling, which acted as a skid.

The big horses had to be led a quarter mile to a grassy little meadow. There was nothing for grazing critters to eat in a forest matted with six inches of resin-impregnated pine and fir needles. The men went through to the final fringe of trees a couple times each day to see how the horses were making it. There was no bigger coward on earth than a horse; this highland country was the territory of cougars and bears, two varieties of critters who were always hungry. And also were meat-eaters. All those four draft animals would require to flee from the highlands at top speed would be either the smell or the appearance of a mountain lion or a bear.

When Gabriel had the saw sharpened to his satisfaction he ambled off to look at the horses. Rick was still filing out that notch in his limbing axe. He watched the old soldier fade out through the trees and smiled to himself. Gabriel had his croaker-sack-wrapped jug suspended from a tree limb there.

The day was better than half spent, the dratted gnats, deer flies, May flies and their annoying companions continually harassed the younger man, shade or no shade. Maybe a blue-tailed fly would not go where it was dark, but there were plenty of other winged creatures who would, and among them deer flies stung when they bit.

So did little critters Indians called 'no-see-ems'. Rick finished with the axe then swung it against a downed fir, the bark flew, he was satisfied and settled in shade to tranquilly await the return of his partner.

He didn't have his pipe along for the

best of all reasons; this late in the year the forests were like tinder, as were the grasslands. This time of year smokers observed natural cow-country law, they chewed, which is what Rick did as he sat comfortably waiting.

He was pleasantly tired as he sat surveying the logs yet to be cross-cutted into manageable length for loading. They would finish up tomorrow, barring something unforeseen, hitch up and drive back the way they'd come.

Rick napped. Afterwards he had no clear idea how long. He straightened up, jettisoned his cud and slapped at a biting insect. He did not own a watch and because it was always shadowy in a forest he had no idea how long he had slept nor what time of day it was, except that it was afternoon.

Nor did he really care, except that his stomach thought his throat had been cut, so he arose, dusted off and went to gather twig wood for their supper fire.

He did not light the twigs within their stone ring, he looked around, saw no sign of the old soldier, and decided Gabriel had probably also fallen asleep over yonder near the little meadow. For a fact, under the circumstances when a tired human being sat down in heavy shade and pine-scented heat, he fell asleep.

Rick drank deeply from one of their canteens and went in the direction of the small meadow. The air was without movement, the afternoon was as still and silent as death. There was not a sound, even tree-top inhabitants, usually noisy this late in the day as they argued over who could perch where, were not squabbling.

This was a small thing, but people living with nature developed the same instinctive awareness animals were born with.

Rick made no sound as he crossed among huge trees, treading a century of mouldering under-story, the topmost six inches of which never rotted and smothered sound until the bottom-most residue was absorbed into the earth.

He came to the surrounding fringe of forest mammoths and halted with a clear view of the meadow where slanting sunshine cast pale shadows outward.

There was no sign of the old soldier — or the big harness horses.

Rick listened to the silence, did not cross out of cover until he had made a quarter-circle of the meadow, found the tracks of his big pudding-footed horses going eastward. He did not have to track them, the imprints would be below the trail of broken, smashed grass all the way to the easternmost rim of big timber.

He leaned against a tree blocking in small areas of the meadow until he saw some rocks with something rocks never had, boots with cotton trouser legs above them partially hidden, and also partially masked by advancing late-day shadows. The boots were heel up, toe down, the natural position of anyone lying face down.

With a feeling of coldness, he retraced his path to the area of the rocks, waited a long time to catch movement across the meadow or hear sound, made a wary approach toward the rocks, which were no more than knee-high and without any trees nearby, in fact with no cover of any kind once a person left the backgrounding trees.

The shock was no more chilling than the expectation of it had been. Gabriel was face down in pressed-flat grass.

Rick knelt to roll the old soldier face up and gazed at the hand he had touched the old man with. It was bloody.

He leaned, looked very closely, finally rolled Gabriel face up and saw where the bullet had struck. Whoever had fired it had been facing the old man; had fired from less than twenty feet. Both wounds, the one entering and the place where it had exited, were bloody, ragged holes. For the old soldier who had survived bullets as well as a bayonet slash which had left an awesome scar, in battles where cannon fire, thousands of yelling men, screaming horses, rifle fire had been deafening, death had come in a tranquil setting of trees, meadow-grass, where a busy small creek made the only sound.

Rick rocked on his heels looking eastward. They hadn't had to kill the old man, he was not armed, neither of them wore weapons when they were working, their gunbelts and holstered Colts were hanging from tree limbs back at the camp.

He leaned slightly because shadows were thickening. Gabriel had probably been sitting perfectly at peace on the rock which now had his blood on it. He had most certainly seen the man whose tracks were in the grass as he approached on foot. Maybe the killer had called a greeting, had been smiling.

At that distance a blind man could not have missed. Gabriel had to have seen it coming. Regardless of how fast the killer had been, the old soldier had maybe three seconds, maybe longer, but he had seen it coming.

Being a sound sleeper had its disadvantages; Rick had heard nothing. The distance between camp and the meadow was not very great. He had slept through the sound of a gunshot.

It occurred to him that the horsethief had not known there were two of them. He had seen an old man sunning himself on a rock, had assumed he owned the big horses and had shot him.

It hadn't been necessary to kill Gabriel. He could have struck him over the head and left him tied — but of course the old soldier had seen the man up close.

For Rick everything orderly had fallen apart. He spent the rest of the day digging the grave. It was too dark when he finished for a burial, so the next morning an hour or so short of sunrise he returned to the rocks, rolled Gabriel in his blankets, settled him comfortably in the hole as though he was asleep, and worked two solid hours covering and mounding the grave. After that he dawdled at the camp for a while. One thing was paramount; he had one hell of a long walk ahead of him if he returned to his ranch. Even if he chose to follow the horsethief's tracks, he still would have a lot of walking to do.

He decided to go tracking, but it required another half hour to hang everything but pots and pans in trees. If he hadn't done this every salt-hungry varmint in the area would chew the leather off the harness, among other things. He left some of their food on the ground. If he was lucky varmints would be content with that. If he wasn't lucky the next time he saw his leather harness there'd be precious little left but the rivets.

He left Gabriel's old Union-issue long barreled sidearm hanging where the old man had put it, buckled his own outfit into place and struck out across the meadow where dew was drying, and had little trouble picking up the sign and following it. Fourteen-hundred-pound draft animals left tracks even over *caliche*.

The country easterly was heavily timbered, and that helped too; pudding-footed horses made imprints in fir and pine needles it was easy to follow.

What he hoped very hard was that the horsethief, thinking he had shot the only person around back yonder, would not be in the customary hurry of most horsethieves.

The country was up-ended, heavily timbered, rocky in some places and steep in other places. The man riding one of his big horses and leading the other three was no greenhorn; the best way on earth to tucker horses, especially the kind that did not ordinarily go up and down mountains, was to make them go in a straight line.

This man angled around slopes, kept pretty much to high ground, and considerately left muddy creeks where he had allowed the horses to drink.

Something about tracking any animal is that the longer a tracker reads the sign, the more the tracks reveal something about the creature being tracked.

For example, the thief kept to shadows, avoided places where the horses had to climb, even halted for an hour or two so they could graze off a grassy marshy little meadow where mosquitoes arose by the millions.

Only once did the thief tie the horses and climb atop a huge rock to study his back-trail. Evidently because he saw no pursuit, when he got back astraddle he seemed to be watching for a camp site. At least he passed up no opportunity to seek those rare places where sunlight reached through the overhead canopy.

Rick Telly was no exception among

stockmen; when it came to walking, especially in rough country, he rested often. This of course put him behind his prey, but to a breed of frontiersmen who didn't even go fishing because it couldn't be done from horseback, foot-transportation, being something they inherently avoided, was not only hard work, it was unpleasant.

He kept at it though, despite frequent respites. For one thing, confident he could overtake the horsethief in time, he did not want to walk up-onto the man while there was daylight.

If he had known what lay ahead . . .

Once, coming around a rough, rocky place, he came face to face with a two-hundred pound black bear. They were both too startled to move. Rick picked up several rocks to pelt the bear with. The bear, no more than two or three years old, reared up on its hind legs and wrinkled its nose.

The first rock missed but the second one struck the bear in his exposed soft parts. He dropped down on all fours and whined.

Rick bent for another rock but the bear, like all his kind, quick to associate the bending with a rock, turned and went in a pigeon-toed gallop into the nearest timber.

Rick gave him ten minutes, then hiked along on the pudding-footed tracks.

The timber did not thin out, but it eventually yielded to lower country which Rick could see by failing daylight. It ran for miles. There was a crooked wagon-road through it that appeared to come from the northeast. It was a well-used thoroughfare.

His horse tracks led directly toward a long-spending drop where the timber stopped mid-way toward the flat, open country.

Those twin ribbons of deeply scored ruts were what people called 'traces'. Emigrants had used them for thirty years.

He went down as far as the final

stand of timber, sat on a deadfall and traced out the horse-tracks going directly toward six or eight circled emigrant wagons where smoke was beginning to arise from within the circle where supper was being prepared.

2

The Wagon Camp

THE horsethief had never deviated from his course toward that wagon camp, nor had he appeared to worry about pursuit after killing the old soldier. Only once had he sought a high place to scan his back-trail.

The thief who had killed Gabriel had thought the old soldier was the only one up there. He'd been unable to see the camp from the meadow. His conviction that he had eliminated the only person at the little meadow with the big horses, was in Rick Telly's favour.

As he sat watching the circled wagons below and ahead some distance across the grazing country, he wondered about those emigrants. He had not got a reliable count of wagons until shortly before dusk. There were six, not seven or eight of them.

Six wagons usually meant at least two people to a wagon, but that could be an incorrect tally; commonly wagoneers had an old relative or youngster along, but whatever their number, the nearest town with a lawman was Crested Butte and it was nine miles from Ricks ranch and from up where he was sitting at present, it was at least twice that far, maybe farther. But if it had been only two or three miles, reaching it on foot, waiting for a posse to get a-horseback and returning for his horses and a murderer, could not be accomplished before daylight tomorrow, which meant the horsethief — all those folks down yonder — would see an armed body of riders approaching for a long time before they came up.

Either the wagon people were some kind of vagrant tribe or the horsethief among them would leave the wagons as soon as he saw armed men heading his way.

There was a third alternative but Rick Telly failed to consider it. What he knew for a fact was that a murdering horsethief had taken Ricks horses as far as that wagon camp down yonder.

There was a scimitar moon, the nights this time of year were not cold until just before dawn. Visibility left something to be desired as Rick started down toward the grass country, using as his sighting flames and shadows where the wagons were.

He needed to reconnoitre; he intended to recover his horses regardless of what he'd have to do to accomplish it, but the purpose of circling wagons in open country was to provide a corral-like area from which livestock could not escape.

As for the murderer, Rick made no decision. For one thing among those emigrants down yonder, the murderer could be anyone. The only way to find out who he was would be to ask questions, which Rick did not intend to do. Right now he wanted his horses back. The rest of it could wait until Rick rode to Crested Butte for help from the law. One thing about wagon trains, they barely more than crawled.

The scent of cooking food and hot coffee reached him from a half mile out. He hadn't eaten since breakfast, and having to bury Gabriel, he hadn't eaten as much as usual.

He knew very little about emigrants. He had seen trains of wagons pass over the years, had paid little attention, and because his cow outfit was distant from the nearest town, well northwest of the trace wagons used, his contact even with emigrant out-riders had been minimal.

He was close enough in darkness to watch people moving within the wagon circle, women, men, a few children. Horses and mules were also inside the circle. There were several supper fires, the largest of which reflected light off a nearby wagon with a soiled canvas cover stretched over ash boughs. At this fire a number of men sat smoking and talking.

What Rick required was a good sighting of his big horses among the other large draft animals.

He was careful to approach the camp from its far side; there was light breeze which would carry his scent only if it shifted. Wagon trains had dogs; it was a matter of speculation whether dogs would make a distinction between his scent and the dozen of other scents.

He squatted in tall grass once when a barrel-chested man walked out of the circle in the direction of a small arroyo and disappeared down into it. The arroyo was parallel to Rick. He waited for the man to re-appear, which took longer than Rick expected. The barrel-chested man returned to the circle, climbed over a wagon tongue which had been made fast beneath the wagon in front, went toward the men at the largest fire and sat on a chair that appeared even in poor light to be the worse for wear.

Supper fires were being allowed to dwindle. They would be fed to provide light but clearly they would no longer be required for cooking.

Someone played a sad song on a mouth organ, someone else took it up with a badly out-of-tune fiddle. This camp was probably like dozens the emigrants had made on their crossing, nor would there be many more trains of wagons because the railroads had been linked up in Utah at Promontory Point. From now on only the poorest emigrant would use wagons.

He could make out silhouettes of big horses but not their colour or markings, so he moved closer, close enough to hear a harassed woman warning her children what would happen if they didn't crawl in their wagon and bed down.

Several men at the council fire drifted away. Clearly, with no crisis to resolve, this after-supper council lacked the urgency of other councils the wagon-men had sat through.

Rick was less than a hundred feet in the grass, able to see inside better, even to make out the colour of some animals, when a lithesome woman left the circle walking directly toward him. All he could make out was that she was slim, had a good stride, and her uncovered head seemed to reflect a pale sheen.

She moved fast. He got flat down to roll, otherwise she could not avoid seeing him unless she changed course, which she did not do.

His first roll was slow, as was his second roll. He did not expect her to see him nor detect movement because the grass was tall and moderately thick. What he was particularly careful of was not to make noise. She was far enough from the circle so that noise from that direction was little more than a murmur.

He was about twenty feet south of her, watching but not particularly worried, when the woman stopped and stood like a rock.

She stood like that for a minute, then leaned slightly peering at the ground. Tall grass was good cover, but pressed flat very easily under weight. Rick held his breath.

She turned in his direction. In poor light all he could make out of her face and figure was that she was young, had blonde hair clubbed someway in back, and stood now with her mouth slightly open.

He waited, hoping — almost praying — she would decide the pressed-flat grass had been made that way by an animal.

She twisted from the waist looking back toward the lighted circle. If she called out . . . Rick could not risk it.

He came up off the ground in a smooth movement which she saw from the corner of her eye and yanked abruptly around facing him.

The musicians back yonder were barely audible. Rick knew the stance of fear when he saw it, and spoke very quietly.

"Lady, I'm not goin' to hurt you. Just stand easy and please be quiet."

She watched him come closer poised to flee. He spoke again in the same quiet tone. "I got a reason for being out here. It most likely don't have anythin' to do with you folks . . . Will you listen?"

She barely nodded her head as she clasped both hands across her stomach. They could see each other clearly when he stopped walking. She was very pretty; he guessed her to be maybe eighteen years old.

Actually, she was close to thirty.

He explained about the loss of his four big horses without mentioning the killing. He described the animals after explaining that he had tracked the horses to the wagon camp. As he was speaking it crossed his mind that the horsethief could just as easily have continued eastward. It had been too dark by the time he got this far to see tracks leading past the wagons.

Her first words settled that possibility. "Two large sorrels and two large roan. About nine years old."

He nodded. Once more she glanced in the direction of the wagons. When she faced him again she said, "Do you know a man named Aaron Copeland?"

Rick shook his head. To his knowledge he'd never heard the name before. "No ma'm."

"He joined us as an out-rider several hundred miles back. He's a stocky man with reddish hair and bad teeth."

Rick nodded; he was not interested in hair nor teeth but evidently she was.

"We had some horses go lame several days back. Aaron said he would scour around and buy replacements. He came into camp just ahead of sundown with two roans and two sorrels, big, powerful horses. Everyone was delighted. Aaron said he'd bought them from a freighter on the far side of those westerly hills. He said he'd given forty dollars a head for them. My father, Mister Barkley, a widow-woman named Oakly and Mister Holfield, each bought one of them."

Rick considered the handsome woman. She had volunteered her information almost as though none of this concerned her. When next she spoke she said, "Mister Copeland's going to ride out come sunup to look for a settlement. The animals need shoes and the folks need supplies . . . Is there a town nearby?"

"No ma'm, not nearby, but there's a town about twenty miles southeast called Crested Butte." Rick was thinking of the man who had killed Gabriel; he would be the man she had just named. He would like to catch Aaron Copeland after he left the emigrants, but being on foot posed a major problem.

He told her his name. "I'm Richard Telly. I ranch some distance southwest of here. The man who stole my horses set me afoot in the high timber country. I'd like to talk to Mister

Copeland . . . but he'll be a-horseback and I'm afoot."

The woman still stood erect, but her original terror had passed. "If you came to the camp and explained — ."

"Lady, if Mister Copeland is there, who'll folks believe, a man they've known for a fair length of time or some feller who was lying out here spyin' on their camp?"

She seemed to be considering this when a booming voice called from the wagon circle.

"Betts; are you out there!"

She called back. "I'll be along directly, paw."

The booming voice did not call again. Rick said, "You're Miss Betts?"

"No. I'm Betsy Calhoun. Since I can remember my paw's called me Betts. Mister Telly, I'll tie a horse outside the circle after folks have bedded down. There's a spindly pine tree a short ways southward from the wagons."

Without another word she turned and walked briskly back the way she had

29

come leaving Rick wondering — why would she be so cooperative? She had never seen Rick before, probably was sceptical of his story, and all she'd had to do was scream and men would have converged from all directions.

He sat on the ground watching dying fires reflect off wagon canvas. She hadn't even acted surprised when he had told her the sorrels and roans belonged to him.

More puzzling, was the matter-of-fact way she had agreed to provide him a saddle animal upon which he could overtake the man who had stolen his horses — and who had murdered Gabriel.

He wondered if it would have made any difference if he had told her of the cold-blooded murder.

He dug out his square of cut plug, worried off a corner, cheeked it and told himself the sweetest molasses-cured chewing tobacco on earth would never take the place of meat and potatoes.

With all the time in the world until sunrise, he scouted southward until he found a sickly pine tree exactly where she had said it would be.

Instead of feeling satisfied, he worried. What he knew about women-folk a man could put atop a harness rivet without causing crowding. He *did* know from books that they could be as sly as coyotes, that they rarely did something like this one had done unless they had a very good personal reason.

He felt no need for sleep. He worried around all the corners of his dilemma. He would get his horses back, that was a damned fact. One way or another he would recover his animals.

It was the brisk, seemingly detached way the handsome woman had agreed — no, had volunteered — to help him catch the man she had said had red hair and bad teeth.

He recalled her without effort. She was very attractive, did not pack an extra ounce of heft, had an almost crisp way of speaking — once she was no longer afraid — and to top it all off, she had figured out a way Rick could catch the horsethief without any prompting from him. After which she had walked back the way she had come without so much as glancing back.

He did nap a little, but each time he awakened he had the same riddle to wrestle with. It occurred to him that she might tie a horse out for him to take — and have the menfolk from the train lying out in the grass to nail him the moment he got astride.

It was a possibility, he told himself. He did not want to believe a woman that attractive would do anything like that, but as some books had said, because women could not match men in muscle they had to manipulate them, or out-smart them with wiles.

He sat against the spindly pine gazing northward where dying fires were down to coals. Occasionally he heard men call back and forth; they would be night-guards no emigrant train was ever without.

The sickle moon moved, the balmy summer night began to get a little chill around its edges. Some cruising coyotes had evidently picked up the scent of a wagon camp. As they hurried past they sounded. Six or eight coyotes could sound like two dozen.

Rick thought about Gabriel, recalled some of the stories the old man had told him of the war. He would miss Gabriel; three years together had forged a good, clean bond between them.

At times the old soldier had treated Rick as a son. Despite their employer-employee relationship when Gabriel saw Rick do something wrong, he would not hesitate to bawl him out.

Gabriel hadn't talked much. He never mentioned personal things. But he had a sense of humour. He also had an amazing depth of understanding.

With the moon well down Rick lifted out his sixgun, checked it for firing order, blew dust off and holstered it. If he became satisfied the red-headed man the handsome woman had described was indeed Gabriel's murderer he would kill him.

A chill came which made Rick wish he had brought along his coat. It wasn't doing any good in the 'possible' box attached to the side of the stripped-down wagon.

He reflected on the camp, the downed timber, the old wagon back yonder in the uplands. There was very little chance someone would find the camp. Even so Rick had left items up there it would be difficult, and costly, to replace. But before he went back up there he needed big horses on the wagon-bed, laden with logs or not.

A dog barked in the northward chilly night. A swearing man made the barking stop.

Rick examined the horse dozing beside the tree. It was a run-of-the-mill animal, built for neither speed nor, noticeably anyway, for endurance. It was a docile bay which Rick determined by opening its mouth was seven years old. There was nothing particularly outstanding about the animal.

The saddle was one of those old-time Texas A-forks with looped-through stirrup leathers and a duck-bill horn. He wondered whether it belonged to Betts Calhoun. It had a narrow tree, which was common to women's rigs, and it was light enough for a woman to toss over an animal's back.

He decided it did belong to her. He wondered what she would tell her father in the morning when — and if — he missed the rig.

Several dogs barked. This time no one growled them into silence. Rick freed the horse, snugged up the cinch, turned the animal a couple of times and swung across leather.

Visibility was still poor but he did not rely upon seeing the out-rider, he remained still and quiet, listening.

The horse coming southward moved

easily, as though he was being ridden on slack reins.

Rick concentrated on what could be heard. The approaching rider would pass the pine tree about a hundred yards westerly.

3

A Long Night, A New Day

RICK was raising his rein-hand when he heard the second horse. It was farther back, so far to the rear of the first horseman in fact, that the foremost rider could only have heard it if he, like Rick, had been sitting still.

Rick swung to the ground, which would make it less likely he could be sky-lined, and listened. The foremost rider was plodding along, his small noises making it difficult to hear the second rider who, it seemed, was trailing the first man by being very discreet about it.

Several thoughts went through Rick's mind: It was the handsome woman, it was someone intending to scout with the man up ahead, but was in no hurry to catch up, it was a personal enemy of the first rider.

He was wrong on all counts.

Rick remained in place, allowed the foremost rider to pass. He was too distant to be more than a moving, indistinct shape in the darkness of pre-dawn.

It was little satisfaction, but he waited until the follower had also passed before mounting and riding westward, pausing often to listen before proceeding, until eventually he heard the second rider somewhere on his left. He sat a while, allowing the follower to get farther down-country before reining out in his wake, and maintaining the distance so that he would not be detected unless the follower halted, in which case he still might not realise he was being shagged — but chances were that he would realise it.

The foremost rider began angling southwesterly. The way Rick made this determination was the way the man he was following also changed course.

It began to appear that while the wagon-train's out-rider had left the camp riding due south, perhaps so that if he was seen leaving folks would know he was heading in the general direction of Crested Butte, he actually had some other destination in mind.

Neither of the riders up ahead increased their gait, which worried Rick; with dawn approaching he would be unable to keep this up without being seen.

The southward run of land was grazing country. If there were trees or thickets they would be few and far between.

He considered overtaking the man ahead of him, throwing down on him if he could, and finding out just what in hell was going on.

Nothing wrong with that idea, unless the man he was following heard him closing the distance, and was the nervous type who shot first and looked second.

The first soiled streaks of dusty red

appeared off in the east. What light showed was neither very strong nor brilliant, but this was a temporary condition. Within another hour the sun would jump up from beyond the farthest curve of the world and within seconds daylight would banish all shadows and night-mists.

Rick was watching for a deep arroyo, of which there seemed to be very few, when he could see the foremost rider turn almost due west. His follower did not follow that course for half a mile. Rick was less interested in the men ahead than he was in the fact that shortly now one, or both of them would see him on their back trail.

The foremost rider passed down into a wide, shallow swale and rode up the far side. His follower did the same.

When Rick rode down the near slope he decided that desperate needs required desperate measures and swung to the ground reaching for his handgun. He intended to hit the bay horse on the poll, which would render the animal unconscious in seconds. As he moved to do this the horse turned a docile eye, waited until the man was even with his left shoulder, then sprung his joints as though expecting a signal.

Rick poked the horse in the shoulder with his gunbarrel. The horse folded his legs and went down on his belly without hesitation or even any noticeable anxiety.

Rick was surprised even as he understood; this bay horse had either been broken to lie down so kids could climb on him, or perhaps so some handicapped person could mount him, but however and why-ever he had been trained to do this, for Rick Telly it was a godsend.

He left the horse, legs folded under like a camel, crept up the far slope and watched the distant riders.

With sunlight exploding in all directions he waited for the first horseman to notice that he was being followed.

The foremost rider did not once look back.

Rick lay a long time, until the other riders passed in among a jumble of immense prehistoric rocks, and did not re-appear on the far side.

They had met. They were together up ahead, whether friends or enemies would be shortly made manifest; if they were enemies there would be gunfire.

There was none. In fact dawn was so silent Rick could hear a rock martin chirping in the distance.

He crept back to the bay horse, tugged him to his feet, rode south for as long as the arroyo lasted, then moved up out of it to flat land, continued riding southward, did not look back for a long time, but eventually he finally did, confident that if the men in the rocks had seen another horseman, this one riding away from them, they would assume it was someone's range rider.

Eventually he turned eastward and rode with the sun in his face until he could no longer see the rocks before changing course again, this time riding in the general direction of the wagon camp.

His original plan had been knocked into a cocked hat, but in its place there was a new mystery. Since those two men had intended to meet among those huge rocks over yonder, why hadn't they simply ridden together?

If the one he had never been close enough to see whether he had carroty hair was scouting for a town, there sure as hell wasn't one in those rocks, nor for that matter in that direction for over a hundred miles.

Maybe the handsome woman had mentioned Crested Butte, and then again maybe she hadn't, although when the first rider had appeared before dawn he was riding in approximately the correct direction.

He halted with the wagons barely in sight, dismounted and pondered. His particular predicament was a lot less healthy. For openers he was riding a horse that did not belong to him, and after two days he looked soiled, unshaven and would appear villainous to people who might be wary of strangers.

He took a long chance, now that it was daylight, rode the horse back to the sickly pine tree, tied it and walked in the direction of the same distant hills he had come out of.

It was not the cleverest thing he had ever done, walking in full view of the wagon camp across grassland where moving objects stuck out like a sore thumb, but the alternatives were just as puny. He expected to be called to, but by the time he had been walking for a quarter of an hour he could not have heard yelling.

What he ultimately did hear was loping horses.

He stopped, turned and stood his ground as three heavily armed men, one the large, massive bearded man he had seen cross from the camp to that deep arroyo the night before, walked their horses to within fifteen feet, halted and sat like expressionless carvings saying nothing.

"My name is Richard Telly," he told them. "You bought four draft horses that were stolen from me a couple of days back."

The massive man gazed at his companions before speaking to Rick. "Are you a freighter?" he asked.

"No. I run cattle across those mountains behind me an' down in grazing country beyond."

Again there was long silence. The next emigrant to speak wore one of those flat-topped black hats with a stiff brim rarely seen among rangemen. He was tall, thin as a rail and had a perpetual expression of resignation which fitted the way he spoke when he said, "Brother, that don't explain what you're doin' over here on foot."

Rick had no intention of explaining why he was out here on foot. He said, "I was wonderin' if you gents are horsethieves, or if a horsethief sold you my horses."

"You come all the way from them mountains on foot?" asked a grizzled, aging man with squinty eyes and a long, hooked nose."

Rick ignored the question. His intention was to protect the handsome woman. "If a carroty-haired feller brought you those horses an' you paid him for them, you might want to know he murdered an old man who worked for me. We were makin' winter wood in the high country. The horsethief shot Gabriel where he was sunnin' himself on a rock — unarmed. Shot him from maybe ten, fifteen feet away. My guess is that the horsethief saw one man watching four horses on a little meadow, figured he was the only person around, an' because he figured to steal the horses, he killed the feller he figured owned them."

The big bearded man spoke again. "You better come back to camp with us mister. That red-headed feller you accused of horsestealin' an' murder happens to be our out-rider. We can all just set down in the shade until he gets back. He's scoutin' around for a town. We're bad off for supplies an' horseshoes. He'll be back maybe tonight, depends on if he finds a town . . . Is there one around here?"

"Crested Butte, about a day's ride from here. But gents, that's not where your out-rider went. Him an' some feller who trailed after him. They went south for a few miles then bent around westerly an' met in some rocks about eight miles from where they turned west."

This time the silence ran on so long Rick was beginning to wonder if they'd ever speak. The older, hooked-nose man with faded little narrowed eyes did not address Rick, he spoke to the massive, bearded man. "Well now, Mister Calhoun, we either got one hell of a good liar on our hands — or — Mister Copeland's turnin' out like some of us suspected for the last couple hunnert miles."

The bearded man studied Rick.

"How do you know Mister Copeland went all them places? Mister, you're as good as tellin' us you followed someone — you on foot, them a-horseback — maybe ten miles or so."

Before Rick could answer someone at the wagon camp began beating a large pan. The noise was clearly audible where Rick and his companions were standing in tall brome grass.

The massive man whose features were impossible to read because of his bearded face, lifted out his sidearm, shoved it into the front of his britches and extended a hand for Rick to use in mounting behind the rider.

That was how they rode back among the wagons where women sweating under an overhead sun were feeding fires and preparing a meal. All movement seemed to cease as the riders entered the circle and swung to the ground. Rick looked for, and failed to find, the handsome woman with the taffy hair.

The horses were led away by round-eyed youths who had seen the riders overtake the walking stranger. The smooth-faced individual with the flat-crowned black hat went to a log and sat down. There were several old chairs around this particular ring of blackened stones. Rick had seen the man palavering here last night.

The men who had returned with Rick had evidently thought hard about what he had said, because as they trooped over to also sit, not a word was spoken.

A wisp of a woman with unkempt grey hair, furtive dark eyes and a long, sharp nose approached the bearded man, leaned and whispered in his ear.

She walked away as the massive man turned slowly to regard Rick. He said, "Mister Telly — you didn't walk after those fellers last night, did you?"

Rick returned the older man's gaze without blinking and did not reply.

The massive man abruptly arose and strode in the direction of a wagon near the lower end of the circle. The other men watched. One, the slitty-eyed, hooked-nose man said, "Somethin' roiled him up, for a fact."

The man sitting beside Rick made a wry comment. "It don't take much, Calvin."

The resigned-looking individual arose, nodded and departed. Rick was left with two older men. They did not look at him. Elsewhere, the camp was noisy, fretting animals who had eaten all the grass inside the circle down to dust, milled hungrily. Rick saw his four big horses. He had never liked to see hungry animals, but today his animals were nuzzling dust for grass shards right along with the other animals.

The hooked-nose older man got a cud tucked into his cheek and offered the plug to Rick, who shook his head as he asked a question. "Did another rider leave here about the time Copeland did, real early this morning?"

The older man exchanged a look without answering. The second man stuffed a foul little pipe, fired it up and the smell of half shag, half kinikinnick spread.

The narrow-eyed older man considered the activity around them, mostly farther southward from the palavering site, and gently wagged his head. "Sure as we're settin' here, Martha Oakly put a bee in Calhoun's ear. That woman . . . I'd guess she never sleeps an' can out-hear a Missouri mule. I wonder how her husband ever put up with all that gossip. A man can't take a leak she don't know whose wheel he peed on."

A gangling youth who bore a striking resemblance to the handsome woman with taffy hair came over to say a meal was ready any time the seated men cared to eat. As he was walking away the man with the pipe knocked dottle from it and arose. The other man remained seated. They exchanged a nod which left Rick with only one companion as the hungry emigrant strode in the direction of several long tables near a cooking fire.

The hooked-nose man put a steady gaze on Rick, almost smiled and spoke quietly. "The trouble is, Mister Telly, your story sort of fits with some other things. Mister Calhoun's wagon master. He's got to make the first suggestion about what folks should believe, then we pass a vote . . . I can make a pretty good guess how you followed Mister Copeland . . . I went out early an' saw Betts Calhoun's bay horse tied to that poorly-lookin' pine tree." The old man spat aside before continuing. "My guess is that the widder Oakly saw it too, an' that's what she whispered into Mister Calhoun's ear . . . And that could be interesting — for instance, how did she come to tie that horse out there rigged for riding, and what her paw'll sure as hell want to know, how come her to know you."

Rick gazed at the older man, who appeared to be about the same age Gabriel had been. In other ways he reminded Rick of old Gabe.

The older man, having gotten no response to his earlier remarks, smiled a little, arose to go eat and lightly slapped Rick on the shoulder. Before walking he made a calm statement.

"If you'd of just come into camp . . . Well, I guess then we'd never have known about Aaron — that feller you figured was following him, is a man named James Curlew. He joined us back on the Missouri. He had good stock and a good wagon. He told Mister Calhoun he'd hunted and trapped most of the country between the big river and the Dalles up in Oregon. He's some sort of French Canadian. Mister Telly, I've met my share of them folks an' to be real truthful about it, they never set well with me. But I got to tell you Jim Curlew's a good man to have on a wagon trip."

"Was he and Copeland close?" Rick asked, and got a thoughtful head shake by way of reply as the older man walked away without speaking. Rick looked after the older man who put him strongly in mind of Gabriel.

The gangling youth who resembled Betsy Calhoun ambled over, smiled and sat down. He was quiet for a spell then said, "My paw's madder'n a wet hen."

"What about?"

"Betts helpin' you last night. They got into it somethin' fierce. Betts got a temper. So has paw. He never liked her husband, but I did. Well, but paw had tears on his face when we buried Alfred back among the brakes on the Missouri."

"What did he die of?" Rick asked.

"Blood poisoning they called it. There was some Mormons back there. One of 'em was a doctor. Big, hefty man. He done everythin' he could, poulticed Alfred, purged him, used some special Mormon medicine made from bushes; paw said no doctor ever worked harder . . . But like the Mormon said, once blood poisoning gets hold of a person, they die."

The lad looked briefly at Rick before looking away. He was by nature a gentle, shy youngster. "My name's Patrick. Patrick Calhoun."

Rick held out his hand, the youth pumped it once and let go as he arose. "You'd better come eat, Mister Telly."

Rick followed the lad over where milling, noisy emigrants were eating. Some but not all the noise diminished at his arrival. Old Calvin Stuart winked between mouthfuls.

4

Preparations

THE heat did not abate. As afternoon advanced several mounted, armed emigrants took the livestock out where there was better feed, and a piddling little warm-water creek.

Betts's father returned to the council site where Rick was watching his four big horses out yonder. They were cropping grass like there would be none tomorrow.

As the wagon master sat on one of the rickety chairs he and Rick exchanged a nod but no words until Calhoun fired up a pipe whose stem was barely long enough for the bowl to clear his beard. He puffed up a fair head of smoke, removed the pipe and asked a question. "When you met my daughter out yonder in the dark, it liked to have scairt the daylights out of her. How long had you been out there, Mister Telly?"

"Since shortly after dusk."

"Why didn't you hallo the camp? You'd have been welcome."

Rick shifted to achieve a greater degree of comfort as he replied. "I trailed my horses to within sight of the wagons. If they were down there, then someone among the emigrants had to be the thief. I had no idea what my reception would be if I walked in looking for a horsethief . . . Maybe you know, Mister Calhoun, west of the Missouri emigrants don't have a very good reputation. They've stole, chickens, beef, tools, horses . . . If I'd walked in and said those big horses had been stolen from me, how would I know the whole party of you folks hadn't been stealing horses along the way?"

Calhoun puffed hard to get up another head of smoke — for a

fact smoking a pipe and carrying on a conversation was just about impossible. He tamped ash with a callused thumb and leaned to watch the grazing livestock. "Mister Telly, this feller you told us you tracked last night an' this morning, is our out-rider, has been with us for a month or so. He's not popular, but like I tell folks, we didn't hire him for his likeability, we hired him because he knows the country. We got a long way to go to reach Oregon. Mister Copeland's been there an' back several times. . . . About the horses — it'll be his word against yours. We know him well enough, we never saw you before this morning."

Again the massive man tamped and puffed, got a fair smoke rising and removed the pipe to continue speaking. This time he also gazed far out as he said, "My daughter was a fool; she'd never seen you before." Calhoun paused briefly to expectorate into the dead ash inside the fire ring.

"We had an argument. She told me

somethin' I had no idea about. Aaron Copeland caught her out on horseback, pulled her off the horse . . . " Calhoun paused to expectorate again, puffed, and resumed speaking. "Betts is strong; she can use her fists. She's had to while growin' up. They scuffled. She caught him unguarded and knocked him down. She got on her horse and came back . . . That was some time back. Since then she's avoided Mister Copeland." The massive man lowered the pipe, gave up on it and turned to face Rick. "She said she hoped with all her heart Aaron did steal them horses off you." The large man's eyes bored in. "Mister Telly, are you much force with a six-gun, because if you aren't . . . I've seen Aaron Copeland shoot the head off a prairie chicken from the saddle. The rest of us been usin' guns most of our lives, but I don't believe there's another man in this party who can shoot that good. I sure can't."

Rick edged toward some puny shade. The sun was making shimmery waves of dancing heat. He did not answer the wagon-master's question, he asked a question of his own.

"Who is James Curlew?"

"A feller we met back yonder. He had a good outfit and was waitin' for a train to come along so's he could join. Tryin' to cross the country alone is pure suicide. If the tomahawks don't get you, renegades will. Mister Telly, we've run across more bands of renegades than In'ian war parties. Mister Curlew is real handy. He can cobble together broken wheels, fix worn hubs, doctor livestock."

"Is he friendly with Aaron Copeland?"

"Well; until we listened to you, I'd never noticed them together very much . . . Now, folks are divided. Either you're a real good liar or you're not, an' if you're not, why then Aaron and James Curlew meetin' out in some rocks don't set real well . . . I'll tell you for a fact, even before Betts told me about her run-in with Aaron, I respected his knowledge of the route an' all, but I've yet to invite him to set at supper with me."

Rick was thoughtfully silent for a long moment or two. "Mister Calhoun, the nearest town is Crested Butte, about twenty miles from your camp. Maybe a tad more or less. A man on horseback can cover that much country in a day, if he don't dawdle. Now then, if Mister Copeland shaped his course toward Crested Butte, I'd say he'd ought to be back by tomorrow evening. At the very latest the day after tomorrow."

The massive older man re-fired his pipe and this time did not take it from his mouth to speak. He sat watching the distant grazing animals and their mounted guards.

In the direction he was gazing open country stretched a great distance before butting against a low range of dark mountains.

Rick interrupted the other man's ponderings. "Your daughter's got spirit. If she hadn't offered to help me, I'd have had to walk all the way down to Crested Butte to get help."

The big man turned his shaggy head to drily say, "We'd have still been here. We've had sickness and some of the animals are either lame or so tender-footed we can't move until we get shoes for them."

Calhoun's son came up, stood a respectful distance to tell his father some of the folks wanted to talk to him. As the big man arose to depart his son shot Rick a furtive, shy smile.

Someone, Rick told himself, had told the gangling youth the stranger among them did not bite heads off. He knew who he hoped had said that, but only went as near a wagon as the water-barrel, dippered his full, and sat down in the shade. Now he and the emigrants would wait.

Calvin Stuart came ambling along, shirt dark with sweat, long nose shiny, little narrowed eyes pale in their ruddy setting, shrewd and knowledgeable. He sat down in wagon shade, shared his cut plug with Rick, and spoke a moment later when the younger man remarked on how fresh and soft the cut plug was.

"I got to apologise for that, Mister Telly, but I just don't hold m'water as well as I used to."

Rick spat out the cud, which the older man affected not to notice as he said, "I didn't happen along to loaf in shade, Mister Telly. The reason I come could get my head busted. Betts Calhoun wants you to meet her out back of their wagon come sundown. She'll be doin' some washin'." Calvin expectorated lustily before continuing. "There's somethin' you'd ought to know, young feller, the wagon double-tongued in front of the Calhoun outfit belongs to a widder woman name of Martha Oakly . . . You remember the woman comin' by to whisper in Mike Calhoun's ear at the council ring?"

"Yes."

"Well, son, she's the biggest gossip, has the longest nose for pryin', and the sharpest tongue this side of the Missouri River — which is back where we buried her husband — who went into the ground with a smile on his face . . . Now I just passed that along, because if she sees you two this evenin' and tells Mick, he'll give her what-for then he'll come lookin' for you."

Rick had no difficulty about his decision. He said, "She's a real handsome woman."

The shrewd eyes considered Rick in silence until the younger man also said, "But I'm here to get back my horses an' to settle with the son of a bitch who killed the feller who worked for me."

They continued to sit in warm shade without a word passing between them until big Mike Calhoun came along, paused to regard them before asking if they were conferring or just palavering. Calvin patted the dust. "Set," he told the big man. "Mister Telly was just tellin' me he figures to take back his horses, and to kill whoever murdered his hired man."

The wagon-master did not comment on something that was general knowledge, he mentioned something altogether different.

"My boy went out with the tenders to mind the livestock." Calhoun paused to pick up a smooth, small stone which he examined as he continued speaking. "They drove the livestock to that creek out yonder, an' come onto shod-horse tracks where a fair-sized body of riders had watered there maybe last night. They sure didn't water their horses after daybreak. We'd have seen 'em. Pat said Preacher Spencer sent him back to tell me."

Rick listened and said nothing. Calvin also picked up a small stone, but instead of examining it, he flicked it with his thumb, and watched dust spurt where it landed.

"How many riders, Mike?" he asked.

"They figured at least ten, maybe fifteen." After making that statement Calhoun raised an oaken large arm to gesture with. "Where would those men be? That's open country to the end of the earth."

Rick offered a suggestion. "The only place that many riders could go between maybe midnight an' dawn without bein' seen would be westerly, back the way I came. That's the only cover."

He did not pick up a small stone but he too husbanded some private speculations, one of which was that if those riders went far enough through the mountains they would find — and most likely plunder — his wood-making camp.

Calhoun had a suggestion which he had not tried out on the other emigrants yet. "First off, we're settin' ducks out here. Second-off, we could only move the wagons that got healthy animals to pull them, which would mean the party'd get strung out. Thirdly — don't it seem a band of riders out here miles from anywhere, might wait for daylight to ride on in — to get fed if nothin' else? It worries me havin' strangers movin' through in the night . . . Suppose we

66

made a party an' tracked them, just to be on the safe side."

Calvin's squint became more pronounced as he said, "An' leave the camp exposed? Mike, them men worry me too, but maybe if two or three of us went scouting, everyone else ought to fort-up right here until we get back."

Rick finally picked up a small stone and flicked it. He'd had vague misgivings all day, something he could not define, but it existed.

As he spoke the older men looked at him. "Ten or fifteen riders muddying the creek where you folks tank up the animals, then disappearing in the timber somewhere . . . Suppose they're settin' up there right now watchin' the camp? If the three of us left the camp following their tracks, they'd see us the full distance. If we found them, we might not get back. If we didn't find them . . . What I'm sayin' is that they knew we'd find their marks at the creek. They then went up into the hills to set down and wait." He paused to gaze at the older men. "If they're what you gents are hintin' about, that's exactly what they'd want, only they'd like it better if all the menfolk got astride with weapons an' went chargin' up there . . . There wouldn't be anythin' but scattered tracks, an' somewhere those men would come together, ride down out of where the searchers were lookin' and raid your camp."

Calvin's slitty eyes were fixed on the younger man. "Mister Telly, you ever rode with marauders? Because just now you sure sounded like you had."

Before Rick could reply Mike Calhoun got to his feet looking past the rear of the shady wagon in the direction of the heat-hazed mountains. "I'm goin' for a walk. If they bypassed the camp last night headin' for them hills, they left sign. Even over hard pan that many shod horses would leave sign."

Calvin said nothing. Rick offered an admonition. "Mister Calhoun — they're watching. Most likely they're lyin' up there right now, watching. If you go out yonder lookin' for tracks, they're goin' to know why."

The massive older man turned, frowning. "We got to know, Mister Telly."

"Why? We already got a real good suspicion. If I was in your boots I'd go through camp quietly gettin' folks organised and ready for an attack. If they come, we can empty some saddles if we're ready, if they don't come . . ." Rick shrugged.

After Mike Calhoun departed old Calvin continued to sit slack and thoughtful. Eventually he said. "Mister Telly, I don't want you to take this wrong because I don't mean it that way — but you put me more'n more in mind of someone who's been around marauders before."

Rick smiled a little. "Mister Stuart, the feller who worked for me, the one someone killed back near our camp up yonder — well — sometimes winters are hard in this country. Old Gabriel an' I'd set around the stove swappin' lies. He told me quite a bit about the war. Mostly how the Rebels had to figure a lot because they was out-numbered most of the time. They tracked Yankees. Their speciality was ambushing. Lots of times they'd lie low an' watched Union men march past; then track 'em at night, set up their ambushes and kill as many as they could before reinforcements came up. They'd run off through the woods and start planning their next hit-an'-run."

Calvin sighed. "Mister Telly, I was in the Union army from Bull Run to the last scraps durin' the Peninsula Campaign."

Calvin turned with a sad little smile, slapped Rick on the leg, arose and walked away.

The heat did not diminish, some of the water barrels were getting low. The wagon-master organised parties to go over to the warm water creek, fill up and return. Rick noticed that every man in the water party was armed to the gills. Evidently Mister Calhoun had decided in favour of Rick's suggestion.

When dusk was close he went over to be fed. This time he saw Betts Calhoun with a sweat-shiny face helping cook and serve, and she saw him. They exchanged a long glance.

He went among the contented livestock, which were now as full as ticks and willing to remain cooped inside the wagon circle. All they'd need until tomorrow would be water, of which there was now plenty.

There was not quite as much noise as people ate and afterward, as there had been before, something else Rick noticed.

As dusk settled he took a position opposite the Calhoun wagon, easily distinguishable even as dusk thickened, and was unheeded by emigrants who were beginning to worry about being attacked at night.

Men were cleaning guns, women were putting everything that might be trampled inside the circle, either under wagons or inside them.

Rick wondered if the watching raiders had spy glasses, something he was confident, from Gabriel's stories about raiders and ambushers, they would have, and was satisfied that with dusk induced minimal long distance visibility they would be unable to discern the obvious preparations for defense inside the wagon ring.

Mike Calhoun came along looking harassed, paused to mop off sweat before saying, "You ever been in this kind of fight before, Mister Telly?"

"No, never have."

"Well; you might have made a pretty fair soldier."

Rick smiled. "I doubt it, Mister Calhoun. I was never much good at takin' orders."

Calhoun walked in the direction of his wagon still mopping sweat. Rick saw him climb inside, and only moments later climb down on the off side heading northward, outside the circle but close to the wagons.

Betsy Calhoun climbed out of the

wagon stepping from seat area to the hub, and from there to the ground. She turned directly toward Rick and crossed over, seemingly indifferent to whatever glances might be turned in her direction.

She had her taffy hair pulled back in that sort of horse-tail braid, her dress fitted loosely, her stride was, as Rick would learn, distinctive to her; long steps, smooth, muscular movements.

Once she turned in the direction of a wagon behind, saw swift movement where the widow Oakly had abruptly pulled back from peeking around the puckered canvas of her wagon, resumed her crossing until she slackened pace as she said, "Good evening, Mister Telly," and smiled at him.

He nodded. "Good evening. I thought our meeting was supposed to be sort of a secret."

"It was, until paw climbed in a few minutes ago and told me you were over here, if I cared to talk to you." Her smile widened. "That's the first time since we left the bottoms where my husband is buried, that he didn't snarl when men came around."

Rick said, "Care to walk a little outside the circle?"

"Well — paw said to stay inside, but — ."

"Then we'll stay inside."

She turned. "Follow me."

They returned to the Calhoun wagon, but in front where the wagon tongue was chained to the next wagon to complete the corral-like circle, she climbed over the tongue, turned and as he did the same she took him around the side of the wagon where there were two battered wooden benches. She sat on one and he sat on the other.

The moon was nearly full. It had a rusty appearance because dust rising from the earth this time of year made an almost impenetrable, invisible overcast.

5

'Walk!'

"**D**O you really think they are out there, Mister Telly?" she asked, gazing in the direction of the heat-blurred uplands.

He considered his reply before offering it. "If they went west, they'd reach that high country, an' they sure enough would like forest shade after the kind of daylong heat we've had lately, and if they're raiders, they'd most likely want to set up there where it's cool and look down this way."

She smiled at him. "I like your direct answers."

He smiled back. "All right. I plain don't know but I think they are up there."

"Why would they splash across the creek and leave tracks?"

75

"So's a bunch of curious emigrants would follow the tracks."

"And?"

"They'd lead them a far piece into the timber, circle around and come down here, raid the wagons an' be gone before the emigrants could get back."

She continued to gaze at him, no longer smiling.

"Have you seen this sort of thing before, Mister Telly?"

"No ma'am, but a friend of mine I think your red-headed out-rider killed, told me how those things were done back during the war."

Because she had already heard the story of Gabriel, she did not leave her central topic. "We were attacked in broad daylight in the mountainous country back up north before we came down to this lower country. Only it was In'ians."

"You came through all right?"

"Yes, mostly because there was a company of dragoons at Bridger's Fort.

Someone who heard the shooting told their officer. They came up firing and the In'ians tucked tail and ran."

"Scairy was it, ma'am?"

Her eyes widened. "Scairy? I was petrified with fear. After it was over we buried three In'ians. One of them had a child's blond hair braided into the fringe of his britches."

"Did you lose any folks?"

"No. Only Mister Stuart got cut in the leg. It was a graze but it bled some. The fight was too short or I'm sure we'd have had casualties . . . Mister Telly?"

"Yes'm."

"Where is your ranch?"

He jutted his chin. "Right about where I'm looking. On the far side of those mountains about eight, ten miles. There's a big meadow country over there. There's three other cow outfits, but we're a long way from each other."

"Does your wife like being isolated?"

He looked at her. "I don't have a wife."

She swiftly changed the topic. "We're going up to the Oregon country. Paw heard stories about it from folks who settled out there. It's good farm country with plenty of rain."

Rick nodded. He too had heard stories of the Oregon country. They had sounded alluring but he was satisfied where he was. It had taken him seven years to make his holding the way he had planned. Now, with room for expansion, he planned to take up more ground and increase the size of his herd.

She interrupted his thoughts. "My father figures Aaron will get back maybe by tomorrow night or the next day — if he finds that town you told paw about."

Rick nodded. Clearly her father had been close mouthed about a few things. If that was the way Mike Calhoun wanted it, that's the way it would be.

He toyed with the idea of asking her if she knew Aaron Copeland very well, decided not to because so far their visit had been calm and amiable. Instead, he asked where the Calhouns had come from.

"Illinois. Paw farmed there. His paw did the same before him." She seemed to hesitate before speaking again. "I married Alfred Calhoun who was a distant cousin. It was the custom in my paw's time and his paw's time, because nearly everyone in a farming settlement was related one way or another to everyone else, and also because towns and villages were a long way apart. Too long for courting during the winters when snow piled half-way up the house."

He grinned. That had to be as good a reason as any for folks to inter-marry. For a fact high snowdrifts that hung on for three or four months, would put a crimp in going sparking, particularly if a person had to ride or drive any distance.

His big meadow got snow two feet deep on level ground almost every winter. Drifts could be as high as five to six feet.

She asked about the southwesterly country, which was visibly low and more or less level for hundreds of miles. He told her what he knew, he also told her of Crested Butte, which got its name from a high, flat monolith a dozen or so miles from where the village stood.

Betts Calhoun had been married; she understood some things about men, so she asked if he would like some coffee.

He declined, fished for his cut plug. She watched him gnaw off a sliver and cheek it before she said, "I tried that once."

His eyes widened on her. He'd seen women smoke corncob pipes, even those little crooked, dark Mexican *cigarillos*, but chewing tobacco was strictly a man's area of pleasure.

She looked rueful. "I was so sick I thought I'd die, and wished I would."

He wanted to laugh but didn't. If

80

he had known her better he would have.

She made a sweeping motion with both arms. "The nights are so beautiful; stars by the hundreds, a soft yellow moon, fragrant air to breathe." She looked around at him. "Why aren't you married?"

He almost lost his cud.

"You must be thirty or more."

"Thirty-five," he told her, groping his way after being surprised.

"What's the point of building a cow ranch if you have no family, Mister Telly?"

He'd been too preoccupied the past seven years to think of that. He did not think of it when he said, "I got tired of working for other outfits. I wanted to own the cattle I worked an' the land they grazed over."

She said, "You'll get married someday."

She made that statement with such candid confidence she could safely move on to the next subject. "When

81

will they come — if they come, Mister Telly?"

They were back on firm ground again. He looked westerly. By day's end it was easier to make out details of the forest giants up yonder than it had been during daylong sun glare.

"I got no idea. Old Gabe would but I don't."

"He was your friend, Mister Telly?"

Rick wasn't sure whether 'friend' was the right word. The Mexican designation, *compañero* was closer. "We was better'n friends, Missus Calhoun."

"Will you call me Betts?"

"Be glad to, ma'm, if you'll call me Rick."

"Rick, when Aaron returns . . . " She let it dwindle into silence.

He'd been thinking of something all day that marginally held his attention, but what she had just said inclined him to offer an answer influenced by his thought. He said, "*If* he returns. Him and the other feller."

She looked at him waiting for the rest of it, but he stood up, stretched and said he thought he'd go see how things were going, climbed back over the tongue and disappeared from her sight.

She sat a long time, until a wolf howled out in the ghostly-lighted countryside somewhere, then she climbed into the wagon.

The fires had been allowed to burn down; Calvin's idea was that too much brightness would background the defenders.

Pieces of heavy furniture and some barrels had been placed as obstacles behind the chained tongues between wagons. Rick thought that since this had been done long after sundown, the raiders would have no idea these defenses were in place. He had no idea whether they would charge the camp on horseback seeking a way inside between wagons, or whether they'd leave their animals with holders and try to creep soundlessly in for their attack.

There were several men at the council

site. They had no fire, each man had a rifle or a carbine and every one of them was wearing a shellbelt and holstered pistol.

He walked over there, they nodded as solemn as a bunch of owls. He sat on a round of firewood. The sad-faced man with the stiff-brim flat-top black hat spoke first. "I was just sayin' it's a shame folks kill each other, Mister Telly."

Rick saw Calvin's slitty-eyed amused expression, while seated nearby massive Mike Calhoun ignored the preacher to ask if Rick thought the raiders would shoot the horses, because if they did, the emigrants were likely to have to camp where they were for the rest of the summer.

Rick doubted that the horses would be shot. Live animals had a cash value, dead ones didn't have. He saw Calvin watching him, did not answer the question but asked if the older man would like to make a scout on foot with him.

Calvin jettisoned his cud into the cold ashes inside the stone ring and nodded as he leaned to arise. As he reached for his rifle he addressed Mike Calhoun. "If you hear a night bird call you'll know we've found somethin' an' you gents can get among the wagons with your weapons."

Until Rick and Calvin were clear of the camp moving in the direction of the uplands Rick was quiet, but when he was satisfied he would not be overheard he said, "If you make a bird call or any noise at all they'll know we're out here tryin' to scout them up."

Moonlight was both their ally and their enemy. Visibility was fair; at close range it was excellent. They moved parallel to each other with about a hundred feet separating them.

Rick raised his left hand several times; they would stop and listen. There was nothing to be heard until they were about a mile westward, then it wasn't the sound of horses, it sounded more like nocturnal grazing animals.

But they hunkered in tall grass anyway.

There was no wind, not that they could detect anyway, but abruptly the band of animals up ahead somewhere broke over into a panicky run southward.

Calvin leaned. "Antelope?"

Rick shrugged. As far as he knew antelope did not feed at night. He thought it more than likely it had been deer but that did not hold his attention as much as something else did. He would have bet a new hat those stampeding animals, whatever they had been, had not seen or scented the two hunkering, motionless men a hundred yards or more east of them.

Calvin leaned to speak again. Rick held up a hand for silence. The moon was high and round, the ground had a ghostly tan shade to it, the night was still breathless. Calvin looked twice at his companion. Rick did not move, he was peering ahead and seemed to scarcely be breathing.

Calvin was getting impatient. He

fidgeted a little but remained low against the ground.

Rick was about to give up when he heard it, a man's hoarse voice speaking curtly in soft, indistinguishable sentences.

Calvin froze.

Rick strained to hear what was being said, failed at that and pin-pointed the direction of the voice. He waited for shod-horses to make the soft, whispery sound large animals made passing over curing tall grass.

It was a considerable wait. Evidently the raiders were seasoned, experienced men at their trade, which was murder and plunder.

The horse-sounds were less noticeable as shod hooves than as dry, unoiled saddle leather. Even at a distance on a still night that little abrasive sound carried.

With infinite slowness Calvin brought his rifle up off the ground to rest it crossways on his knee. Even that movement annoyed Rick. Right there he decided that Calvin and Gabriel were not that much alike.

The invisible riders halted. After a long moment a man's distinct words came quietly. "We'll go some closer then leave the horses."

Rick listened to the soft rubbing sounds. When he could dimly make out riders, he counted two. Scouts sure as hell.

He leaned to brush his companion's arm, held a finger to his lips, and wolfishly smiled. The odds were even, with the men in the tall grass having a slim edge. The oncoming raiders did not know they were there, and *they* knew where the raiders were.

The raiders halted again. This time Calvin recognised the speaker when a man said, "Ground-tie the horses, from hereon we go afoot . . . I tell you, friend, that's the dumbest bunch of wagon people I've ever come across."

He got a dry answer from a voice neither of the men in the grass recognised. "They better be. You want to fan out a little? Be better if we snuck up from different directions."

As they prepared to separate the man whose voice Calvin had recognised, said, "Mind now, no noise."

That admonition must have stung his companion; he turned without another word and angled southward. As the other man started forward on a northerly angle, Calvin leaned to whisper. "Jim Curlew — the one that went south."

Rick nodded as he followed the swishing sound of the raider walking toward him but on a northerly angle. He tapped Calvin's arm and pointed in the direction the other man had taken. Calvin nodded and eased up into a crouch to begin his stalk.

Rick did not know James Curlew, beyond what he had heard, and also what he had seen when Curlew and Copeland had met secretly in the rocks.

He could barely distinguish the man angling away from where he squatted. He had hoped it might be Aaron

Copeland, but this man was taller and leaner.

He let the raider get ahead of him and followed as silently as possible. He did not have a rifle or carbine, but if he could get close enough his six-gun would do just fine.

But only if he had to use it. One gunshot would send echoes in all directions.

The lean man strode ahead carrying his Winchester on the left side. His attention was on the ghostly pattern of wagon canvas ahead.

Rick wanted to close the distance, but that idea died instantly when the lean man abruptly halted and looked back.

Rick was flat on his stomach. If the lean man had been closer he could have made out the dark shape by looking down, but for that the distance was too great.

He started walking again.

A horse squealed inside the wagon ring, probably a horsing mare some gelding with fading instincts had nipped on the rump.

Rick was able to close the distance when the lean man faced forward and resumed his way. The distance was close to being good enough for a six-gun. He prayed for that horsing mare to squeal again but she didn't.

They were close enough to the camp to make out details. Rick wondered for a second how Calvin was making out. The lean man violently sneezed. Rick scuttled closer. The lean man lustily cleared his pipe and expectorated. Rick was closer when the lean man fished for a bandana and blew his nose. He was standing with his Winchester balanced against his closed legs when he did this.

Rick pitched two small stones. The lean man jerked erect grabbing for his Winchester. Rick ignored the sounds he could not avoid making in the grass and came to within fifteen feet of the lean man before the lean man whipped around.

Rick cocked his six-gun.

The lean man stared. The surprise had been complete. Rick told him to let the Winchester fall, which the raider did. He then gestured with his cocked Colt. This time obedience was slower, but not even an idiot would try to draw against a cocked six-gun from a distance of no more than fifteen feet.

As the lean man emptied his holster he said, "Son of a bitch!"

They faced each other over an interval of silence before the lean man snarled, "Well, are you goin' to pull the trigger or ain't you? If you do before you can reach them wagons a whole herd of men will ride you down."

Rick gestured downward with the gun. "On your belly an' shut up."

The lean man went down with profane reluctance. Rick stepped over, jammed his gunbarrel hard over the prone man's kidney and repeated it. "*Shut up*! Not a sound out of you!"

He used the raider's soiled bandana

to lash his wrists in back, picked up the man's guns, prodded him to his feet and tersely said, "*Walk!*"

The raider walked in the direction of the wagons.

6

The Wait

CALVIN was already at the council circle when Rick and his prisoner arrived. Calvin looked rumpled and exhausted. He had come up behind his man while the latter was peeing, had knocked him senseless, then had to exasperatedly squat out there until the raider came round, prod him to his feet and because the injured man stumbled and yawed as he shuffled ahead, Calvin eventually had to put an arm around his raider and lead him. It had been a tiring experience. His prisoner sat on a log at the palavering site with his head in his hands. There was blood, but most of all the captive had a world-class splitting headache. For conversation this made him as useless as teats on a man.

94

It was Ricks prisoner who snarled at every question, made dire threats and never seemed to look at anyone, always over their head or slightly to one side.

His name was Junior Quayle. He was disagreeable, he looked scarred and battered, his lipless slit of a mouth had a downward droop, his eyes were tawny-brown and although he looked to be in his fifties, he was actually the same age as his captor, thirty-five.

To every question he snarled the same reply. "I don't know what you're talkin' about, you clod-hopping bastards."

Mike Calhoun sat hunched forward gazing at the lean man. He was no taller than the raider but he easily out-weighed him by a hundred pounds of muscle, sinew and bone.

Everyone in camp knew Mike Calhoun had an Irish temper. The men around the stone ring with him remained silent, waiting.

Calhoun's voice was silky-soft when

he said, "Mister Quayle we got women an' children. Your friends out yonder tackled the wrong set of wagon-people this time . . . I'm goin' to demonstrate to you how dead serious we are . . . Rick, untie his hands."

As Rick leaned to jerk the bandana loose the raider studied Calhoun. With a gun he might have stood a chance, hand-to-hand he didn't stand the chance of a snowball in hell, and he understood that, but by nature he was unyielding.

When his hands were free he rubbed both wrists looking slightly past the wagon master. As he began to lean he said, "I got a rock in my damned boot."

He did not have the opportunity to lean very far. For all Calhoun's heft he was as quick as a cat. He bowled the lean man off his log, landed atop him and drew back a ham-sized fist. The raider, startled but able to recover quickly, turned his head aside as the big fist caught him a grazing blow on the side of the head.

Junior Quayle arched to throw Calhoun off; there was too much weight bearing down on him. He tried bringing up a knee as he slashed viciously with both fists. The blow alongside the head had evidently done no damage.

Calhoun absorbed the lighter man's blows, smothered most of them by leaning forward, grabbed the raider by the throat with his right hand and fended off the stinging blows as much as he could with his left hand. He exerted pressure with a hand wide enough to reach both sides of the raider's throat. He had learned this hold many years earlier when he had half-strangled a bully. He had no idea what the process was but he did know if he exerted enough pressure and held on long enough, an adversary became unconscious, which was what happened with the man beneath him; he went as limp as a wet rag.

The preacher said, "You broke his neck."

No one made a sound as Mike Calhoun got to his feet, punched his shirt back inside his trousers, leaned and with one arm hoisted the raider to his feet.

The lean man blinked, tried to move but could not, and looked around into the bearded face of his adversary.

The fight was out of the man. Calhoun took him back to the log upon which the raider had been sitting and pushed him roughly down. He then resumed his seat across the stone ring and said, "You're lucky, Mister Quayle; usually when I choke a man he dies." It wasn't the truth but it had the desired effect.

The lean man gently massaged his gullet, and this time he looked directly at the wagon master, but not immediately.

"I don't know nothin' about anything. Me'n that feller with his head in his hands been travelin' through. We figure to go down where they're findin' gold an' — ."

Mike Calhoun interrupted by slowly arising with balled fists. For seconds those two looked at one another. No one else moved or made a sound. Calhoun gently wagged his head. "You had your first lesson, Mister Quayle. Now — the second one'll end with you havin' some broken bones an' maybe a cracked jaw."

The reply was quick and venomous. "You over-grown ape, there's thirty raiders out yonder sneakin' up to surround your camp. All I got to do is holler."

Calhoun opened his right hand into a half-closed claw and started moving. Suddenly, the injured, half-sick renegade said, "You damned fool, Junior. He'll make mincemeat out of you. You ain't goin' to holler an' there ain't no thirty men out yonder."

Silence descended, the man Calvin had struck over the head lowered his face to his hands again. As far as he was concerned, all his defiant companion was going to do, was get them both either killed or the next thing to it. Right at this moment if silver chariots drawn by pure white horses surrounded by men in white robes playing on golden trumpets suddenly appeared in a dazzling light overhead, he would not have raised his head.

Massive Mike Calhoun remained standing. Junior Quayle would not look at him as he said, "They're comin', you can bet on that. Him an' me was to scout, return an' lead the raid."

Calvin jostled the man he had captured. "Mister Curlew, where is Aaron?"

Without lifting his head the injured man spoke through his fingers. "Up there. Out yonder with the others . . . He talked me into this, the son of a bitch."

Calvin asked one of the spectators to go fetch the jug from his wagon. The preacher went to place both hands on the shoulders of the injured man as he spoke reprovingly to Calvin Stuart.

"You didn't have to hit him so hard, did you?"

Calvin twisted to look up. "No, I expect I didn't have to, Reverend, but I wonder how many folks you've read the Good Book over who didn't hit hard enough."

Mike Calhoun addressed the defiant man. "How many raiders are there?"

"I told you — thirty!"

The move forward and the blow itself was a perfectly coordinated effort. For the second time the lean man went backwards from his seat, only this time he did not move.

An old man whose straggly beard was white and whose face was deeply lined, chuckled. Otherwise the silence lingered until the injured man spoke through his fingers again. "Mister Calhoun, you can half skin him alive. He won't give you the time of day."

Calhoun returned to his seat, sat hunched with big hands clasped and gazed at the man with the bloody head, shoulders and shirt front. "How many raiders, Mister Curlew?" he asked.

"Ten, countin' him an' me."

"How did they happen to be out here, Mister Curlew?"

"Ask Junior."

"I'm askin' you."

"Him and Aaron Copeland sized up your train miles back. Aaron got you to hire him on as a scout. The idea was to lead you to this big prairie with mountains to the west an' the nearest town twenty miles away."

Mike leaned back. Around him silent armed men solemnly considered the injured man. Calvin, sitting beside Curlew, poked him with an elbow. "An' do what, James?"

"What do you think, Calvin? I told you, Aaron talked me into joining. I never done anythin' like this in my life."

"Why, Jim? Hell, you been travelin' with these folks a long time. They treated you well an' all."

The man leaning with blood-stained clothing holding his head in both hands said no more until the jug was brought from Calvin's wagon. Curlew lifted his head long enough to drink deeply, then lowered it again as the jug was handed to Mike Calhoun, who took it over where Junior Quayle was lying, propped the raider against one massive leg and poured whiskey until the lean man coughed, flung his arms, coughed more and spat, and finally turned to look at the bearded face and the thick arm holding the jug.

Mike Calhoun's expression beneath his beard was solemn as he raised the jug. Quayle tried to fend it off using both arms, but it kept coming. Quayle squawked and threshed until he fell back to the ground. The oaken arm kept coming. Calhoun placed his free hand around Quayle's throat. "Drink! Two swallows or I'll break your neck."

Quayle took three swallows, flung his head sideways and gasped. Calhoun let him up, gravely handed the bottle to Calvin and returned to his seat across the fire ring.

Reverend Spencer looked more disillusioned than ever but he kept silent, and eventually turned his back on the others.

A heavy-set short man addressed the wagon master.

"If they was sent to scout us an they haven't got back . . . "

Several men nodded. Calhoun looked at Rick Telly, who looked back and made a small shrug. It was anyone's guess how long the raiders would wait for their scouts to return, but it was also likely that when their scouts did not return, they might turn wary. Might even ride away, which Rick doubted.

The bull-built short man said, "We got until daybreak, only I wonder if they'll hang an' rattle that long?"

There was no answer to that question, unless their prisoners could supply one. The injured man raised his head. His eyes looked like two burnt holes in a blanket but only Calvin Stuart was close enough to see this, and he didn't look, but he smiled faintly at the recovery his corn squeezings had affected as the injured man said, "They'll come. You can bet new money on that. They didn't trail you all this way just to turn back."

Rick asked who the leader was of the raiders. Curlew answered without hesitation despite the vicious look he was getting from Junior Quayle. "A feller called Begley. He won't quit. That's his reputation."

"Do you know him?" Rick asked.

"Met him a couple of times when Aaron took me with him. Behind his back they call him Milk Eye. One of his eyes is milky looking. I don't know whether he can see out of it or not, but if he can't you sure wouldn't know it." Curlew paused, met Quayle's glare, looked swiftly away and spoke again. "They're a bad bunch. Aaron pointed out one to me who murdered his own parents. Another one is wanted in Texas for killing two soldiers when he escaped from an army stockade."

"How about Copeland?" Rick asked.

"He's wanted for murder in Kansas. He bragged to me about it. He uses some stuff in a bottle to make his hair red."

"How about you?" Calhoun asked, looking steadily at James Curlew.

The injured man would not meet the wagon master's gaze. He was silent until Calvin poked him again with a bony elbow. "Deserted from the army an' stole that wagon an' the horses."

Mike Calhoun looked briefly at the ground, then shook his head. He had cottoned to Curlew, for a fact the man was handy and had always been obliging and helpful. He arose and left the council area walking in the direction of his wagon. That short, bull-built emigrant said, "It's hell on a man who trusts someone like you, Jim."

After Calhoun walked away there was nothing more said until Rick made a suggestion. The other emigrants had also cottoned to Curlew — all but Calvin; as he'd said to Rick, French

Canadians should be watched.

"We can set here or we can put the boot on the other foot. Gents, if we set here long enough they'll attack the wagons. For all we know they're sneakin' in close right now."

Reverend Spencer mildly asked what Rick had in mind. He replied curtly. "Settin' ducks get killed. With women and children it'll be worse. An old man who used to work for me said at least a dozen times durin' some long winters, defendin' yourself keeps you too busy to win. If you hit first, the boot's on the other foot." Rick stood up and stretched. "Be back directly," he told them and walked toward the east side of the wagon circle where there was no light except that provided by the moon.

The lean raider watched Rick walk out into the gloomy night. "I wish to hell Aaron hadn't stole that son of a bitch's horses."

For some reason that amused Calvin Stuart, who laughed as he too arose to depart. Putting his amused gaze on the lean man, Calvin said that unless he was very wrong, the lean man's friends would wish the same thing before this night was over.

Not everyone would have said that; their assessments of Rick Telly were mixed, mostly favourable to have another gun in the camp, but still mixed.

Rick, like Mike Calhoun, went among the dark wagons on the east side of the camp to pee.

He was returning to the centre of the wagon circle when Betts's brother appeared. He did not have a belt gun, he was carrying a hexagonal-barreled old buffalo rifle that shot a slug as large as a thumb pad. He looked uncertainly at Rick, who said, "Good evening. If you hit anyone with that gun they'll be wolf bait."

The gangling youth made a feeble smile. "I'd feel better if I didn't have to fire it. Do you figure they'll come?" Before Rick could reply Pat Calhoun also said, "Paw come to the wagon a while back brooding about something."

Rick understood; as that short, heavy-set emigrant had said, it was hard on a man who trusted and liked someone to discover they deserved neither trust nor friendship. "He's got a lot of responsibility on his shoulders, Pat. Do I think they'll come? Maybe. When their scouts don't return they might tuck tail and run — but from what I've heard, they won't do that. How is your sister managing?"

"She's got more guts than a tanyard pup. She put all our heavy furniture an' boxes on the near side of the wagon. She gave me paw's old buffler gun, a pocket full of slugs for it, an' I never seen her wearin' a shellbelt an' pistol before. Not even that time a couple of months back when some In'ians attacked the train."

Pat paused, "The bullet belt an' pistol belonged to her dead husband. I got no idea whether she knows how to use a gun."

Rick grinned. "My guess is that she can use it."

The lad strolled on his way, he had been told by his father, who had organised, an inside patrol, to make a round of the camp, as he'd instructed other men to do. He had told them to particularly pause between wagons and look hard for movement out in the night.

Rick watched the gangling youth continue his patrol. His impression was that Betts had inherited her father's resourceful toughness, and maybe her brother had inherited a different kind of nature, possibly from their mother.

Reverend Spencer came along. Rick asked where his gun was. The man whose expression reflected disappointment in mankind lifted his coat aside. A six-gun with beautifully carved walnut grips rode low in the holster.

Rick raised his eyes to meet the dead-level gaze of the preacher. He said nothing; he nodded as the minister walked away.

Life was full of surprises. That had been a weapon someone had taken exceptionally good care of. Someday, if he had an opportunity, he would like to spend a little time getting to know a preacher who not only carried a six-gun low on his right side, but whose gun carried beautifully carved grips, things which had mute implications.

He went looking for Calvin. During the course of his search he met the dowdy, sharp-featured Widow Oakly. She told him Mister Calhoun had detailed Calvin and several other men, to go out into the night, lie down and listen. If they heard or saw anything they were to hurry back inside the circle to sound the alarm.

She raised a short arm and pointed to a brass bell atop the Calhoun wagon. Rick was certain the bell had not been up there earlier.

He walked to the Calhoun wagon, rattled gone-dry wood with his knuckles, waited until Betts poked her head out.

"I heard you forted-up inside the wagon."

She stepped over to the driver's boot and straightened around to climb down, something Rick watched with interest and approval. When she turned he smiled. "You look like Missus Jesse James."

"Does he have a wife?" she replied. "I've used the gun before, at jack rabbits as we drove along, once at some wild dogs."

"Did you hit them?"

"No, but I was close enough if they'd been as large as a man, I would have . . . When will they attack, Rick?"

He had no idea. He was convinced they *would* attack, but had to guess about when and how. "Before daybreak," he told her.

"That's a long wait."

He agreed. "But your people are ready, as ready as they'll ever be. Your paw's got patrols inside and scouts outside. Everyone, even your brother, has a weapon. Betts, my guess is that when they arrive someone is goin' to get one hell of a surprise."

He was correct but not in the way he meant.

7

The Real Surprise

MIDNIGHT came and went, the silence was deeper now than it had ever been. Rick completed his circuit of the forted-up camp, sat down on one of the rickety chairs at the fire ring and gazed across it at Junior Quayle. There were several other men sitting in long silence, among them was that short bull-built emigrant. He was examining a loaded Colt. When Rick arrived he holstered the gun.

Junior Quayle sneered at Rick. Those three swallows from Calvin's jug had at least for the time being, heightened his contempt. He said, "Why in hell did you buy into a fight alongside a bunch of wagon people?"

There was an easy answer, which Rick gave, then pointed. "Take off your right boot."

Quayle did not move but the men around him did, they stared at the renegade as understanding arrived slowly.

"*I said take off your boot!*"

The stocky emigrant lifted out his six-gun without haste, pointed it and cocked it.

Quayle leaned to tug up his trouserleg and remove the boot.

An old man with white whiskers leaned to retrieve the boot, he peered into it, put a hand inside and pulled it out holding a short-barreled under-and-over derringer with a big bore.

The husky man holstered his six-gun and looked daggers at the renegade. Quayle glared back. "You never seen a hideout before, Clod hopper? When you been out here as long as I have you'll learn stayin' healthy makes a person want to cover every bet."

The old man tossed the derringer to Rick, who shucked out both loads and pitched the little gun among the ashes within the fire ring.

The burly-built man arose and jerked his head. "I got a log chain that'll keep you for a while."

As before the renegade made no move to obey. "I'll remember you," he told the burly, short man.

The reply he got for that threat was given in the same hostile tone of voice. "I sure hope you don't forget me, you worthless son of a bitch. Get up!"

This time Quayle arose. The others watched the husky man herd his prisoner in the direction of a nearby wagon.

The old man with the white beard said, "He'd as leave shoot him as look at him. I seen him when them In'ians attacked us. He's a dead shot with a handgun."

An emigrant snug inside a wolf skin jacket came over to say Mike Calhoun wanted to talk to Mister Telly.

Rick found the massive, bearded man hunkering on a small wooden keg between two wagons. Calhoun was rubbing a six-gun with his bandana handkerchief. He looked up as he said, "We're ready inside. Cal Stuart and two other fellers is out yonder on the west side. I'd like for you to join me goin' out on the east side. I know, you figure they'll come from the west. I figured that too, but I also got to wonderin' — thinkin' like I figure they might think — since their scouts didn't return, they'll wonder if maybe we didn't get hold of 'em. If so, why then they aren't goin' to charge us from the direction we caught their scouts, are they?"

Rick did not answer. He leaned on a tailgate gazing out into the ghostly-lighted easterly country. Calhoun holstered his weapon and stood up. "Care to come along? If you'd rather stay in the circle I can find another man."

Rick faced the older man. "They got eight men, how many have you got?"

"Fourteen, countin' men an' boys."

"Mister Calhoun, if you can keep 'em from gettin' inside, it'd be better. You've got women and children inside. Raiders don't leave anyone alive if they can help it."

The big bearded man stood gazing at Rick until a glimmer of an idea arrived, then he said, "You think we should all go out beyond the wagons?"

"Maybe not all; leave some inside just in case, but the rest of us would do better if we could stop 'em from getting close to the wagons."

"We don't know which way they'll come, Mister Telly."

"No, but if you string men completely around the wagons out a ways, we'll hear or maybe see them, an' the word can be passed along."

Mike Calhoun took his time replying. He did not like the idea of stripping the inside of the camp of men. He thought Rick's idea would have had merit if there had been twice as many emigrants as there were.

"Let's you'n me scout out a ways.

We can talk about this while we're bein' useful."

Rick nodded and followed the large man outside the circle of wagons. He would have traded a good horse to know whether the attack would be made on foot or a-horseback.

The farther they got from the wagons the more night-time stillness and silence engulfed them. There was a faint scent of cooking-fire smoke in the air. There were distant and irregular dips and rises. By daylight the land looked flat. By night-light the low places showed as shadows.

Where Calhoun halted to lean on his rifle, it was as still and empty-seeming as any place on earth. He faced Rick. "We heard of raiders, bands of them, but mostly they was said to be farther west. You heard of them out here before?"

Rick hadn't. "The most I've known of have been maybe two or three men stealing livestock, but where I ranch is a long way from emigrant trails."

The massive man stood eyeing the younger man. Eventually he said, "Well, no sense in wishin' we was back east, is there?"

They squatted in the grass alternately looking forward, on both sides and back in the direction of the wagons.

"There's somethin' I'd like to ask you, Mister Calhoun."

"Go right ahead — ask."

"Did your daughter tell you about Aaron Copeland pulling her off her horse some time back?"

The bearded man's expression changed, but only visibly around the eyes. "She did."

Rick said no more. After a time the older man resumed speaking. "I would have killed him. She said if I did we'd be without a scout in a part of the country none of us knew. We argued. Betts is good at compromising. She said she would carry a derringer from now on if I'd hold off settling with Aaron until we found one of the emigrant roads leading to Oregon . . . Mister

Telly, it was hard. Every time I looked at him I wanted to grab him by the throat."

Rick chewed a stalk of grass without speaking. It worried him having no idea from which direction the attack would come. Mike Calhoun broached another topic. "Jim Curlew's treachery surprised me. I never saw him an' Aaron together very much."

Rick broke his silence. "They'd be careful of that, wouldn't they? My guess about Curlew is that he's like a lot of people — honest as long as it's to his benefit, treacherous when that seems more profitable. Most of all I think he was easily influenced. Whatever else you'n I think of Copeland, he's tough, resourceful, and strong-willed. That kind usually influences the Curlews, seems like."

A night bird called from somewhere south of the camp. Rick scarcely breathed waiting for the answer. When it came it was southeastward, somewhere behind where Rick and Mike Calhoun squatted, between them and the wagons.

Calhoun twisted to listen, turned back to speak when Rick held up his hand for silence.

There was no sound.

Rick swore under his breath and stood up. They were not coming on horseback, they were sneaking in on foot, and they were not coming in either of the directions it had been assumed they would come, they had circled half around far out, anticipating Calvin and others watching to the west, and were stealthily approaching from the direction from which had come the night bird signals, southeast.

He jerked his head and started southward. Whether Calvin and his companions had heard those bird calls and had interpreted them correctly, was going to have to be left to chance.

As they passed close to the circled wagons Rick told Calhoun to go back inside, gather all the men he could spare without interfering with the patrol, and take them to the lower end of the circle.

The massive older man nodded once and walked away. It had occurred to him to ask what Rick intended to do, but with not much time to squander, he had held his silence.

The moon was high, the night was still warm, that faint smoke-scent was still discernible and somewhere among the wagons a horse squealed. That damned horsing mare again. She would be in heat for three days, after that other horses would ignore her.

Rick moved carefully. The moon which had been their ally, was no longer Rick's ally, its dusty brightness would allow him to be seen for a fair distance, exactly as it would allow him to see the raiders.

But he did not see movement at all, nor any dark silhouettes in the grass. He continued southward, pausing now and then to listen. It was as though the area around the wagon camp had been sealed off from the rest of the world.

In a way it had been. It had been deliberately led to this isolated open place where the nearest sources of help were too distant to hear gun shots.

He got parallel with the farthest wagon, hunkered and waited. If they were creeping forward he would eventually see or hear them. Eight armed men could not be entirely silent even in tall grass.

The longer he sat out there the more uneasy he became. He was in the area from which the night birds had called. There should be something audible or visible. With a start he had a searing thought. *They were not out there; those bird calls had been a ruse!*

Ignoring the peril of being exposed he stood up, spun and started for the wagons. They heard him coming, something he did not think of until three men arose out of the grass just outside the wagons and cocked their weapons. "Don't shoot," he called. "It's Richard Telly."

They allowed him to come closer. An

older, lanky emigrant with a prominent adams-apple swore. "You danged fool! You got no business out there!"

A deeper voice snapped at the speaker. "Slack off, Jess." Mike Calhoun climbed over wagon tongues and faced Rick. "You find 'em?" he asked.

"They aren't out there. That was a trick to get you all down here." Rick got over the nearest wagon tongue. The other men followed him. Calhoun grabbed Rick's shoulder. "Where the hell are they?"

His reply did not come from Rick, gunfire erupted at the north end of the circle, most if it coming from massed weapons against a thin, strung-out defiant and surprised handful of emigrants whose return fire was ragged and ineffectual.

Frightened livestock milled, women shrieked, lancing gunflame and thunderous reports broke the long silence as Rick and the massive wagon master led the rush toward the north end of the circle.

They had no targets when they got up there. Muzzle blasts diminished after that first thunderous volley. The emigrants fired anyway and kept on firing.

Patrick Calhoun crawled from beneath a wagon, wringing wet with sweat, his eyes large. He yelled at his father. "Paw, they're goin' to bust in."

Mike yelled back. "Get back under there, shoot at anythin' that moves."

Gun smoke over-rode the scent of cooling supper fires. On the west side of the wagons three men ran hard, leapt over the tongues and turned to help the defenders at the north end of the circled wagons. Only one man did not act completely agitated. Calvin Stuart met Rick and yelled over the gunfire. "We never see anythin'. Never heard anythin'. They must have went far out an' around."

Rick ignored all that to ask Calvin how many guns he thought had been firing out yonder. The older man twisted to look, turned back scowling.

"An awful lot of noise," he said. "Damned if I know how many."

Rick was staring out where the fight had started when he said, "Three or four, firing fast and often." He turned from Calvin to find Mike Calhoun, as he did this he heard a scream at the lower end of the circle and spun in that direction. After the scream there was silence which gradually superseded all the other noise until the last shot was fired and a strange, frightening stillness settled.

People stood like statues. Here and there an emigrant worked at reloading weapons. The short, burly emigrant said, "We run 'em off, by gawd."

No one commented. Mike Calhoun was gazing southward where the penned-up livestock were no longer creating clouds of dust, were beginning to lose their panicky fear.

He turned once, toward Rick, then faced southward again as he spoke quietly to the younger man. "They're inside, Mister Telly."

The stillness was too unnatural; there was dust and strong smells, but there was no sound. The horses drifted to middle ground between the north and south areas inside their circle.

Those who had been reloading now stood with the wagon master and Rick Telly, gazing southward, still braced for battle but there was no one to fire at.

Patrick Calhoun started to speak to his father, Mike said, "Be quiet, boy."

Ten minutes seemed like ten hours. A solitary silhouette appeared down at the far end looking northward. His legs were parted, his right hand held a six-gun, his hat was shapelessly dented, he was a fairly large man.

The silence was stifling. The man down yonder looked up at the crowd of emigrants, just stood there and looked for a long time before he called out. "It's over, gents, unless you don't want it to be, then we'll start shootin' your women an' children."

Rick could feel the tremor pass among his companions. The silence lingered until the stranger down yonder spoke again, his words clear, his tone cold as ice. "You put down them guns, every blessed gun you got, then you walk toward me. Slow, gents, slow with your hands out where I can see them." The voice softened. "Remember, we got a passel of women an' young'uns. First one of you does somethin' mean, we start killin' our hostages. One at a time, your women an' children."

From a wagon mid-way along a soiled, bloodied man called southward. "They got me chained to a wheel."

The man with the wide stance replied only after an interval of what should have been pensive silence. "You let a bunch of clod hoppers grab you? Where's Jim?"

Quayle yelled back. "I don't know. In one of the wagons I expect. He got hit pretty hard over the head. Send me a gun so's I can shoot this chain off."

The distant man had not once sought the owner of that voice. His gaze was unwaveringly on the crowd of armed emigrants. He made no move to do as Junior Quayle asked, he instead repeated his earlier order to the emigrants. "Put the guns down, every damned gun you got includin' hide-outs. We'll search you, boys, if we find a weapon; we'll kill the feller who had it. Now — *put the guns down!*"

Rick dropped his six-gun, the others let weapons fall, rifles, carbines, six-guns, and a few belly-guns, not many of them, emigrants did not ordinarily carry hide-out weapons.

The indistinctly-seen man ahead with the pistol hanging at his side, barely turned his head as he said, "All right, you fellers watch close as they walk down here — one at a time — if any of them so much as sneezes, shoot the son of a bitch." He raised his voice a little. "You hear that, clod hoppers? One at a time you walk down here. Let's start with the big man with whiskers. *You!* Start walkin'."

Mike Calhoun freed his shellbelt and let it fall, stepped over his rifle and began walking southward. The stillness was broken by a horse blowing its nose, although most of the dust had settled by now.

Calvin leaned to whisper to Rick. "We was green as grass. That son of a bitch out-smarted us right down the line."

A man muttered from behind Calvin. "He's had enough experience, I'd guess . . . You got to hand it to the miserable bastard, he's pretty savvy."

Patrick Calhoun was as erect as he could stand, scarcely breathing, his eyes fixed on his father as Mike Calhoun approached the man with the dangling six-gun.

Rick reached to put a hand lightly on the lad's shoulder. He kept it there without speaking.

An old man with a flowing white beard softly said, "I've seen this before. He'll wait, the son of a bitch, until Mike's real close, then he'll shoot him. That's how they make everyone else too scairt of 'em to — ."

"Shut up!" Rick said, and felt the shoulder beneath his hand begin to bunch. He shook young Calhoun slightly and spoke to him.

"I don't think so. He wants a real good hostage. Your paw's the wagon master. He's better'n women and kids."

8

Death and Dust

AFTER Mike Calhoun the other emigrants walked southward one at a time. The livestock was calm, people in wagons peeked out, not even a small child made noise.

The raiders were visible at different places, some half concealed, others in plain sight with ready weapons.

The man who met each emigrant was unwashed, unshaven, had a milky eye and a slit of a mouth. At this time he was triumphant which made him different. He acknowledged every one of his prisoners with a few questions and a jerk of his head. He clearly enjoyed this moment of power. It was not hard to imagine him doing this other times.

When Rick Telly came before the

man he studied him in silence after a hoarse voice called from among the wagons that Rick was the man who had owned those four big draft animals.

The milky-eyed individual's civility was grotesque. He said, "I'm Wayne Begley, cowman. I run stock for years east an' south of here a fair distance. What's your name?"

"Richard Telly."

"Mister Telly, we figured the old man who was watchin' them horses was the only man up yonder."

Rick replied with equal civility — and bluntness. "There was no call to shoot the old man. He wasn't armed. He was just sunnin' himself on a rock."

"Well, the way the story come to me, he had to be killed otherwise he'd have maybe run for help before your big horses could be got back to the train."

"Run for help where, Mister Begley? There's no town, no near neighbours."

"He didn't know all that. Anyway, I'd turn you loose, except maybe for your horses, only I can't very well do that, can I?"

Rick did not reply. Wayne Begley was a big-boned man with a cruel expression. He impressed Rick as also being an individual without nerves or a conscience. Begley jerked his head. "Go stand with the wagon boss."

Two raiders went forward to gather guns. They returned and dropped the weapons. Begley told them to search the emigrants, which they did. Begley then called for the women to come out, when this order had been obeyed he told them to watch the searching; any emigrant found with a weapon would be shot before their eyes.

The night was turning cold, at long last the livestock had enough quiet to be reassured, most of them dozed.

A renegade who wore two guns and a filthy hat with part of the rear brim gone, went up to toss wood into the fires. On his way back he angled toward several women, stopped in front of a budding girl with terror indelibly

135

stamped on her face. He reached for her blouse.

A sturdy woman beside the girl lashed out. The sound of the slap carried. The injured man did not raise a hand to his face, he swung his head toward the sturdy woman as he felt along his shellbelt for a knife.

A raider laughed from among the southerly wagons. Several more laughed. Rick held his breath. Derision often acted as a goad, the renegade had his knife moving forward and upwards when a piping voice called to him from the puckered-closed canvas of the wagon behind them. "Get away from my mother'n sister!"

The boy was no more than twelve years old. He was holding a slingshot fully extended. Wayne Begley spoke. "Ramon, leave it be. Boy, climb down out of there an' stand with your maw." As the renegade moved sullenly away and the child climbed down, Begley addressed the terrified girl.

"You can go with Ramon. He's a real nice feller. He's got a little sack of gold rings and whatnot."

The girl leaned against the sturdy woman, she was too frightened to speak. Behind the leader of the renegades Mike Calhoun spoke.

"You can have our money."

Begley faced around, "Sure I can, wagon master. An' your horses, an' your guns'n ammunition, an' anything else we want, including that girl an' your other women." Begley and the massive, bearded man faced each other, trading look for look.

Begley addressed his companions. "We got until daybreak. Suppose we have a nice hangin' beginning with the wagon master. You boys hoist a wagon tongue an' tie it back. Tie that bushy-faced son of a bitch's arms behind his back."

Two men appeared from where they had been leaning behind barricades of trunks, barrels, pieces of heavy furniture. One had a pigging string

137

in his hand as they approached Mike Calhoun.

That old man with the flowing white beard spoke shrilly to Begley. "Leave him be, you want a victim — take me. My ball of wax is about run out. You want to lynch someone, I'm willing."

Begley twisted to face the old man, raised his dangling six-gun and shot the old man through the middle of the chest. He watched the old man collapse with a soft sigh, turned back and snarled at the man with the pigging string. "*Tie him!*"

Calhoun put both arms behind his back with knotted big fists. Condemned to death he had nothing to lose. He said, "Put up the gun an' free my hands, we'll settle things man to man."

Wayne Begley laughed, strangely he had a pleasant laugh. "If I had to, I would, but wagon master I don't have to."

The two men behind Mike Calhoun remained there after binding his wrists.

Wayne Begley holstered his six-gun, fished for a plug of molasses-cured, gnawed off a piece, cheeked it, spat once and regarded Mike Calhoun. "I want you to feel good before you're sent off . . . Your out-rider was one of us. So was another feller in your company. They brought you out here in the middle of nowhere on purpose."

Calhoun snapped back. "We know all that."

Begley was unmoved by the defiance in the wagon master's voice. "Mister Calhoun, you ain't a real smart man. You let your wagons get drove where there's no way in hell they'll leave this spot." Begley paused, looking squarely at Mike Calhoun. "You'd have a lot of dead folks to answer for, if you was alive. Folks'll remember your name as the feller who let his wagon train get wiped out."

No one moved or made a sound. The only sound came from up near the north end of the circle where that horsing mare squealed again, lashed out with both hind feet and struck a wagon box.

She was ignored as several renegades broke the circle of wagons sufficiently to get a wagon tongue free. They raised it almost straight up after running a length of hard-twist rope through the hame-holder at the tip of the tongue, had a short discussion about the correct angle or tilt to maintain, resolved that quickly by tying the tongue fast to a front wheel of the wagon on both sides. It was as good a gallows as could be devised where there were no trees, and in fact was established procedure among emigrant trains when a hanging was to be accomplished.

Dawn was close, people stood close to each other, some crossed their arms, those with coats buttoned them to the gullet. In one of the wagons a child cried through a blanket.

Across from that wagon a renegade climbed down from a wagon holding a soiled rag to his face. It was the first time Rick or any of the others had seen Aaron Copeland since he had disappeared.

Wayne Begley asked a question. "Why didn't you knock her over the head *first*?"

The burly man with carroty hair dunked his rag in a water barrel before answering. "I did, that gawddamned woman's got a skull of cast iron. She come at me like a catamount . . . I hit her on the jaw."

Begley considered Copeland for a moment before speaking again. "Fetch her out here, Aaron. Pour water over her. She can watch us hang the wagon master."

Copeland saw the upraised wagon tongue with a man below it making the wraps for a hangman's noose. He seemed to forget his bleeding cheek as he bounded back up the side of the wagon.

Copeland was strong, but navigating the climb back out with an inert woman over one shoulder was difficult and delicate work. None of the other raiders moved to lend a hand. Copeland's leaning body as he propped Betts against a wagon wheel hid sight of her but when Copeland stepped clear a woman gasped, and Rick's body stiffened its full length.

Her mouth was smashed, blood trickled, her clothing had been torn, she leaned there looking like a badly treated broken doll.

Her father strained hard against his wrist bindings. A renegade standing behind him stepped farther away, as though expecting the massive man to break free.

The pigging string held.

Calhoun looked directly at Wayne Begley. "Untie me. I only want Copeland. Then you can tie me up again."

Begley made his pleasant laugh and shook his head. "I want her to see this. Aaron, splash cold water over her."

As the man with the red hair looked for a bucket Junior Quayle growled from where he was still chained,

"Wayne, you're wastin' time. Daylight's coming."

Begley turned, regarded Quayle for a moment, then told the man standing behind the wagon master to free Quayle, otherwise he ignored the chained man.

Another renegade growled. "He's right, we're wastin' time an' daylight's coming."

Begley turned on the speaker with a snarl. "We can waste the whole damned day, there's no one within miles of this place, you know that, so shut up."

The emigrants had been silent, wary and watchful, but enough time had passed for them to fear less and think more. Disheveled, grey, sharp-nosed Martha Oakly regarded Begley. "Leave her be an' I'll tell you where every one of us got our valuables hid."

Begley gazed at the shifty-eyed older woman. "We don't make trades, old woman. When she comes around we'll let her watch her paw strangle to death — then we'll work on you, an' you'll

143

tell us where money is hid or we'll roast the bottoms off your feet."

Martha Oakly shrank back among the emigrants. Her place was taken by a tall, raw-boned plain woman with steely eyes. "They said you're wastin' time; let old Martha show you where the valuables are first, then hang Mister Calhoun, it'll only take a few minutes an' you can leave before sunrise."

Begley regarded the tall woman. "What's your name?" he asked.

"Ellen Humphrey."

"You got a husband, Missus Humphrey?"

"Yes."

"Point him out to me."

The tall woman raised an arm. She pointed to the dead old man with the flowing beard. Begley looked, looked back and said, "he's more'n likely your father."

The woman spoke clearly. "I'm not pretty an' he wasn't young."

Begley grinned at the tall woman without speaking.

Aaron Copeland returned with a pail

of water which he took over where Betts Calhoun was propped, hauled back and flung its contents into her face. Watered blood from her smashed mouth ran pink down her torn dress. Her father hunched his muscles again, but the pigging string held.

Betts coughed, raised hands to fend off more water, she coughed again, opened her eyes, saw blurs, and used both hands to push water off with as she blinked, coughed and took down a rattling big breath.

She saw the upright wagon tongue, saw her father's arms lashed in back, saw the others watching, and leaned awkwardly to raise herself using wagon spokes as aids.

Her dress was plastered against every contour of her body. Aaron Copeland stood by with the empty bucket. When she was upright he grinned fiercely, turned and spoke to Begley. "She's my share of the loot, remember."

Begley was staring at the plastered dress. He nodded his head, but with

145

no enthusiasm. Calvin Stuart, who had been still until now, crossed over slowly to hand Betts a handkerchief. Copeland growled and Calvin turned slowly, they exchanged a long look before Calvin returned to his place, perpetually narrowed eyes nearly closed.

Junior Quayle walked over rubbing one wrist. His gaze was venomous, one side of his face was swollen. He ignored everyone but Calvin as he said, "Jim's dead, you son of a bitch. His head was busted. I owe you for that."

Both their holsters were empty and Quayle only had one boot. Calvin seemed to consider his answer before giving it, "I'm here; come on any time you're ready."

Begley snarled at them. "Leave it be, both of you. Junior, go help lean on the rope." He jutted his jaw in the direction of a thick man, dark enough to be Indian or Mexican. "Take the wagon master over there. *Move!*"

Everyone, emigrants and renegades, watched the dark man poke Mike

Calhoun in the back to get him moving. Calhoun turned with a snarl, the dark man back-pedaled. Someone among the emigrants snorted derisively. The dark man cursed and punched Calhoun with his fist, whirled him and punched him again, in the back.

Begley growled harshly. "Drag him over there if you got to . . . Aaron, hold that woman's face so's she can't look away." Rick saw people turning, shifting a little to watch, he looked over where Aaron Copeland was approaching Betts warily. Blood had caked on his cheek. Betts ignored him, watching her father being pushed over beneath the raised wagon tongue. She seemed to be scarcely breathing.

Behind Rick someone touched his arm very gently. He did not move as a small revolver was placed in his hand. He stood perfectly still, turned the little gun to position it properly, and watched the men beneath the upraised wagon muscle a resisting Mike Calhoun directly beneath the tongue.

One man reached for the hangrope as three others held Calhoun in place.

Every eye was on the drama beneath the wagon tongue. A sound almost as loud as a cannon startled everyone. It came from the north end of the circle where dirty white smoke arose.

The dark man was knocked headlong, landed on his face and drummed the ground unmercifully with both feet before he died. Blood poured from his chest.

Begley, Copeland and two other renegades fired repeatedly in the direction of the gunsmoke. Junior Quayle yelped and dove beneath the wagon Calvin Stuart was leaning against.

Most of the people were too stunned to move. Begley yelled for one of his men to go up there, find out who had fired and whether he was dead or not, and if he wasn't to kill him. Two renegades started running. One of them fired his gun empty as he ran.

Rick's heart nearly stopped. He remembered seeing Patrick Calhoun slowly inch himself away while everyone had been watching his sister. He also remembered that Patrick had been carrying that big-bored buffalo rifle.

Those guns were single shot weapons. If Pat Calhoun had another load Rick doubted that he would be able to reload, doubted that young Calhoun could have survived the shots aimed in his direction to reload.

He yelled. Wayne Begley spun as Rick fired the little nickle-plated revolver. Begley's eyes widened, his gun arm was coming up, but slowly. Rick fired again. Wayne Begley sank slowly to his knees.

Pandemonium broke loose as emigrants dove toward the place where their weapons had been flung on the ground. Calvin Stuart bent low, hurled himself beneath the wagon where Junior Quayle had crawled. The sound of their battle beneath the wagon could be heard over the noise of men yelling, women screaming, startled and terrified livestock charging in a frenzied circle seeking a way out of the enclosure. Dust rose, renegades fired as they sought cover at the barricades between wagons.

Rick was turning for another target when he saw that short, heavy-set emigrant's hat fly like a bird as a renegade's bullet struck the emigrant in the head.

He ducked for cover, saw Aaron Copeland from the corner of his eye draw and aim at Betts Calhoun, who did not move in front of the wagon wheel at her back. Rick paused, aimed and squeezed off a shot. Copeland jumped and swung around. He was almost directly in front of Betts. Rick's finger, curled inside the trigger guard, stopped squeezing.

Copeland swore at the top of his voice, fired at Rick, missed and was correcting his aim when Betts kicked him hard over the kidneys. That time the bullet went skyward as Copeland gasped, turned in obvious pain. His teeth were bared, his cheek was bleeding again. He brought the six-gun up again with a thumbpad on the hammer when a blind-mad horse struck him. He went down, lost the gun, rolled and as the horse continued on around the circle he was between Copeland, Betts Calhoun and Rick.

Gunfire swelled as re-armed emigrants fired, sought cover and continued to fire.

The renegades fought back fiercely, but with the barricades to protect them, were only in danger if they showed themselves.

Rick used the eye-stinging pall of dust to start edging toward the Calhoun wagon.

Those men who had run north after the first shot was fired, did not return, they kept on running. They had seen Begley go down, the dark man, two emigrants die, yelled briefly to each other and leapt over the nearest wagon tongue to disappear in the night.

9

When the Dust Settled

EVERYTHING that could have gone wrong, had. As many as sixteen or eighteen emigrants who were firing from hiding made it very dangerous for the raiders to fire back.

Tell-tale gun smoke invariably brought return fire. Wayne Begley was dead, the dark man sprawled in a pool of blood, those two renegades who had been sent to smoke out whoever had killed the dark man, had not returned.

The two renegades standing out yonder with Mike Calhoun left him standing beneath the wagon tongue as they ran for cover among the barricaded places between wagons.

Calhoun dropped flat. As long as the fight continued anyone standing upright could be killed either on purpose or by accident. In either case he was just as dead.

In the pandemonium Rick Telly ducked beneath the front running gear of a wagon, shot his little gun empty, dropped it and peered in the direction of the Calhoun wagon.

Dust was thick. He could vaguely see the fore-wheel where Betts had been standing. He could not see it distinctly, but he could make out that no one was standing in front of it.

He needed a six-gun. He thought Copeland might have made Betts Calhoun duck under the wagon with him. He did not believe he would climb into the wagon.

The nearest visible six-gun was out where Begley lay dead. There was no protection out there. A running man regardless of his speed and zig-zagging course would never survive reaching Begley, taking his weapon and running back.

He squirmed the full rearward distance

of the wagon, came to the barricaded opening, hesitated long enough to determine neither emigrants or renegades were hiding there, crawled out on the far side of the wagon and barricade breathing like bellows, used moments guessing which wagon had men inside, decided and sprang up to race for its shelter. He drew no gunfire for a reason, the renegades were among barricades at the southern end of the wagon circle. Where Rick was, he could not be seen from the lower barricades. All he had to hope for was that some agitated emigrant would not shoot him.

He reached the side where soiled, patched canvas was secured to the wooden siding, heard someone moving beyond the canvas, worked his way to the tailgate and called. At the precise moment he did this, gunfire brisked up all around the southern end of the circle.

He gave up yelling, reached the raised and chained tailgate, rose up very cautiously until he could see inside, where it was sooty-dark, and saw a woman pushing crates and furniture to the west side of the big old wagon to provide shelter for a lanky, kneeling man who was reloading a long-barreled rifle.

During the temporary lull he called to the people inside the wagon. The woman heard him, the lanky man was hard of hearing and did not hear the shout.

Rick raised up very carefully until he could see the woman. She looked haggard and frightened, she put both hands to her face when she saw the wild-looking man peering over the tailgate. She removed both hands to cry out when her husband snapped the rifle chamber closed and moved to re-position himself for firing. He too saw Rick, started to swing the gun, had a thumb ready to cock it, recognised the man at the tailgate and lowered the gun as he yelled. "Climb in. We can use another hand."

Rick climbed over the tailgate. He

said he had no gun and needed one. The woman remained petrified as her husband pulled a six-gun from his waistband and held it out. He had a second six-gun in a hip-holster. Rick spun the cylinder to determine the weapon was fully charged, yelled his appreciation and went back over the tailgate.

In the east there was a smidgen of light but until the sun arose visibility would remain poor. Gunfire slackened, then stopped altogether. Everyone was frantically reloading.

Rick retraced his steps, got back to the running-gear-end of the wagon he had first ducked under for safety. The dust was still over there, but nowhere nearly as dense as it had been.

There was no sign of either Betts Calhoun or Aaron Copeland.

The area between Rick's wagon and the Calhoun wagon was a killing-field for exposed individuals. If he crawled over there by utilising the undersides of several wagons, he had one chance in ten thousand of being able to crawl past one of the barricades where most of the renegade gunfire was coming from without being detected.

Gunfire was being resumed, but with only intermittent shooting. Rick did not even consider trying to reach the Calhoun wagon during this lull. Eventually all gunfire ceased. The silence which followed was as loud as the noise had been, in an altogether different way.

A man yelled from somewhere among the wagons on the west side. Rick recognised the voice. Calvin Stuart offered the renegades a chance to toss away their guns, which, if they did the emigrants would not kill them on the spot but would take them to Crested Butte and hand them over to the law.

The answer came after some delay. It was not derisive, as Rick had expected it to be, neither was it conciliatory, it was plainly spoken.

"We're goin' to pull out an' go for

our horses. We ain't goin' to shoot. We ain't goin' to bother you folks no more. All you got to do is stay where you are for half an hour. If anyone sneaks out to watch us leave, we'll come back. If we get shot at, we'll fire the wagons."

Calvin did not reply immediately. He had two other emigrants under the wagon with him. They had heard the fighting under there and had crawled under in what probably had been the nick of time. That renegade who had fought with Calvin was stronger and younger. One of Calvin's rescuers had stabbed Junior Quayle in the back with a ten inch knife of which only the hilt showed.

Another man called from the southern end of the camp. This one sounded anything but beaten. "Hey, clodhopper, you agree to what was just said or not? If you turn it down I got two kids with me. I'll blow their heads off."

An emigrant called back to the second raider. He had been stung by

158

the raider's attitude. "Mister, you harm a kid, an' we'll fight you until you're out of bullets, then I'll personally tie the hands of each one of you behind your back and drag you to death behind a running horse."

Rick scarcely breathed. He expected a raider to yell back in defiance. Instead, the first speaker called out, his voice still resolute.

"Farmer, you want to end it the way I said?"

Calvin got no chance to reply, someone else did. "It's a trade. Get a-horseback an' don't never come back. No one's goin' to spy on you or shoot."

There was a long lull during which that horsing mare squealed again. She and the other livestock were together near the north end of the compound. The dust had settled and the sun was up.

The strange silence was almost as frightening as the gun-thunder had been. There was no more yelling, just the silence, the oncoming fresh morning sun, and a lot of hungry livestock milling.

Rick looked in the direction of the Calhoun wagon. No one was beneath it and no one appeared from inside it. He had a bad feeling, but he still dared not cross toward the wagon.

The sun climbed, people began to cautiously appear, guns at the ready. Calvin climbed from beneath a wagon and called for Rick. He got no reply for a long time. It was still too early to let the world know where a man was hiding.

Calvin got an answer from over at that wagon Rick had gotten the six-gun from. "He's here somewhere, Calvin. If he didn't get shot he's around here because a short while ago he come to our wagon for a gun."

For a short while there was no more yelling back and forth. That lanky woman who had been married to the old man with white whiskers, went out in plain sight and cut Mike

Calhoun loose. He arose, dusted off and thanked the woman while squinting in the direction of the enclosure. He knew there would be dead, he just did not know how many. There would be some people who would harbour a grudge against anyone who had led them into this mess, not only those who had lost someone.

Whether he had been duped or not, he had done the best he could, his conscience would be clear, moreover, most of the emigrants would split off to go their separate ways once they reached the Oregon country. He would probably never see most of them again — but — as long as survivors lived there would be bitter memories, and since it was human nature to seek a scapegoat, Mike Calhoun did not doubt for one moment who that would be.

The renegades seemed to have been swallowed up by the earth. Inevitably several people went to the west side of the circle to see, but the same craftiness which had allowed the raiders to get inside a defended circle of wagons, helped them now.

Later, people would speculate and advance several theories concerning this, but Calvin Stuart listened to all the tales and rather than spoil them, kept silent.

He had watched the few surviving renegades go north keeping close to the wagons, drop flat in tall grass and become invisible.

He had not seen where they had eventually got back on their feet, nor did he track them out of curiosity, he had more than enough other things to do, such as digging graves, something he abhorred, not because it was hard work, but any man Calvin's age could not look into a fresh grave and not feel a little cold on the hottest day.

Rick and Mike Calhoun reached the Calhoun wagon at the same time. The massive man climbed up, looked in, remained looking in for some time, then climbed back down. "Gone," he told Rick. "The son of a bitch took her with him as sure as we're standin' here."

Rick frowned faintly. He did not believe Aaron Copeland was in traveling condition, he had seen him go down twice, the last time Copeland had been on his feet with a pointed six-gun.

He tried to remember a particular gunshot coming from the area around the wagon, and failed. There had been too much dust, noise and confusion to remember any particular moment.

He did not say a word to Betts's father. He crossed to where the old man with the white beard was lying, picked up a six-gun, flung a shellbelt over his shoulder and was heading for the milling livestock when he saw Betts's brother, dirty, rumpled, hair awry, leaning on a wagon looking northward. He called to the lad, who turned very slowly.

"Did you see 'em, Pat?"

"See who? I didn't see no one."

The lad resumed his former position

against the wagon gazing into space.

Rick was saddling a sturdy buckskin horse when a lanky emigrant strode up carrying a rifle. He stopped to watch and as Rick was cinching up the lanky man said, "Mister Telly, that's my horse."

Rick glanced around. "Would you take a hundred dollars for him?"

The lanky man grounded his rifle and leaned on it. "Where are you goin'?"

"To find Betts Calhoun and kill the son of a bitch who took her off with him."

"Well, that bein' the trouble, I won't sell the horse, but I'd take it kindly if you don't bring him back wind-broke or crippled."

Several people had seen Rick at the upper end of the circle. Calvin was one of them. He and a grim-faced man started walking. They couldn't have closed the distance if they had been running.

Rick led the buckskin out of the

circle, turned him a couple of times and swung across the saddle. The lanky emigrant with the rifle called softly, "Good hunting, Mister Telly," then, as Rick rode in the direction of the mountains, the lanky man saw Pat Calhoun standing like a sleepwalker, and went over to him.

He didn't say a word, he just perched on a wagon tongue, very methodically rolled a brown-paper cigarette, got it fired up and sat almost stoically gazing southward, where people were working at creating order, hauling the dead where they would be out of sight, and the tall woman who was now a widow was helping Martha Oakly get a cooking fire started. The lanky man smoked, looked down there, watched the tall woman for a while then spoke without looking at the lad.

"You know that tall lady down there at the stone ring?"

The lad turned to look. He replied in the same inflectionless voice he had used to Rick Telly.

"I know her. She's Missus Ambrose. Her husband was the feller with the white beard who got killed."

The farmer-type emigrant smoked, watched them down yonder and spoke quietly without looking at the lad.

"It takes a real woman to get back to work with her husband dead only a few hours. Boy, tonight she'll cry her heart out." The emigrant expectorated, turned to face young Calhoun. "Your paw's all right. I got faith Mister Telly'll fetch back your sister. It's all right to feel bad, but other folks is worse off — but they're older'n you an' that makes a difference. Somethin' you might want to remember, partner — nothin' happens that a good night's sleep don't make it more bearable."

Pat blurted it out. "I shot that man! I could see him kicking and flopping, before he died. He didn't even know it was coming."

The emigrant leaned to grind out his smoke before speaking again. "Boy, when you're older you'll understand — ."

Young Calhoun broke across the older man's drawled words to say, "My mother read us the Bible. She raised us up believin' we should obey the Book an' all. That means not to kill things."

The emigrant considered the youth for a moment before speaking. He had deep-set grey eyes and a normally tolerant understanding look. "Boy, listen to me. I was raised up with the Good Book too, an' for some time I had the same trouble you have now. When I was about your age I shot an In'ian who was scoutin' us up all painted for war. I shot him through a place where the chinkin' had come out from between the logs of our house. He blended so perfect with the autumn leaves if he hadn't been movin' I most likely wouldn't have seen. I was shakin' so bad when I eased the rifle barrel between them logs I never expected to hit him. But I did, an' after the noise of a gun goin' off inside brought my maw an' paw, an' they saw what I'd done, I was shakin' so bad my maw took me to the side of the bed and held me real close.

"My paw come back with the In'ian's musket an' knife, which he put on the table, took me from my maw and told me somethin' about God. He said God knows that when the things a man believes in got to be defended, afterwards a man can look up an' nod, an' God nods back. He understands."

The emigrant arose, took Pat Calhoun by the shoulders and turned him. "Now look up an' nod."

The boy obeyed.

10

'It Don't Make Sense'

THERE was no way to cross the open country on the trail of the renegades without being seen by anyone up ahead in big timber looking back, but the alternative of waiting for nightfall to make the crossing was something Rick Telly would not do.

The muscled-up buckskin was strong and willing. He was also, like most short-backed horses, hard riding.

The sun climbed, Rick and the buckskin reached the foothills and started following a zigzag game trail which the renegades had also followed. The closer he got to thick timber, which was ideal ambushing country, the more careful he became.

He had not a single doubt that he had been seen, had been watched, and up ahead somewhere they had prepared their bushwhack.

He left the game trail riding angling along the uphill side of the timberland. If they had seen him, as they certainly had, if they would hunker at their ambush a little longer he might get behind them. Beyond that he made no plans.

He accepted the fact that the men he sought were seasoned renegades and that there would be no ruse they had not either performed themselves or knew about, otherwise they would not have survived this long.

It did occur to him as he made his careful way into the timber and through stands of it, that lacking the experience at this sort of thing his enemies had, he was at a disadvantage. He thought only of finding them, finding Betts Calhoun, and taking her back to the wagon camp.

The sun had reached half way to its meridian. There was heat down where the emigrants were going about repairing what damage they could, but it would remain pleasant in the high country until later in the day. There were areas where a man could ride for hours without seeing sunlight. In places the huge fir trees were too close together for a man to ride between them.

Rick had to guess at how far he had ridden, but any lifelong horseman could do that with reasonable accuracy.

When he thought he might be far enough westward on the sidehill, he eased down toward flatter country, left the buckskin tied and went on foot seeking horse tracks.

He did not find any, which encouraged him to believe he had indeed gotten behind the renegades. He returned to the horse, rode southward for a time, then turned eastward, still believing he might surprise the renegades from the rear.

Timber country invariably has treetop sentries, large, blowsy, noisy blue jays, who monitor every moving thing below and, if their particular home-grounds are invaded by trespassers, they squawk, fly lower, scold, sometimes even make passes at invaders.

This happened as Rick turned eastward, he passed through a particular domain where jays were nestling; they flew over him, squawked, scolded, flapped into the trees to follow his progress, and in general made enough commotion to warn other wild creatures that a two-legged critter was in their territory.

Rick had experienced this many times while hunting strayed cattle. It hadn't bothered him then, but bothered him this time; he had to assume the renegades knew as much, and perhaps more, as he did about hide-out country and the nature of its inhabitants. The farther east he rode the more raucous the jays became, until Rick decided to leave the buckskin and scout ahead on foot.

Aside from the possibility of the renegades hearing and understanding the birds, Rick had only a belt gun, no rifle or carbine. If there was shooting he would have to be close.

The sun climbed, wide-branching tree tops closed it out, back where Rick had left the buckskin jays were concentrating on the horse.

He halted often to affirm his bearings and to listen. He estimated that he was within a quarter to a half mile to the final spit of trees before open country would be visible, and that gave him misgivings. If there had been an ambush he should have come very close to it by now.

He stopped, leaned against a forest monarch, blended with it as he listened, heard nothing and decided to go downslope and perhaps get southward of the renegades.

It was a good thing he did this. He found no tracks over layered fir needles, but he did find where a horse had left droppings.

Without wasting a moment he headed back for the buckskin, whose customary nap when left to stand, had been a total failure because of those swooping birds.

The renegades could still have an ambush in mind. Whether they had or not they had left the game trail riding southward. Why, Rick had no idea; southward would be roughly parallel to the emigrant camp. A considerable distance west of it, but still parallel. Rick speculated as he rode. Going southward the renegades would eventually run out of tree cover. The landforms in that direction all tended, bowl-like, to slant in the direction of open grazing land down near Crested Butte. He thought that, in their boots, he would have ridden west. There was cover for many miles in that direction, few ranches, all of which could be avoided, and beyond, more timbered slopes and mountains.

He had difficulty keeping to the track. Fir needles took impressions, but being dry they did not do it well nor hold the impressions for long.

He thought it was early afternoon, not that it mattered. The farther south he rode the more sign he found, and the more baffled he was, until, with shadows beginning to thicken, the tracks turned eastward.

Rick stopped, watered the buckskin at a measly little creek, and gazed eastward. To his recollection the timber over in that direction only went as far as another grassy sidehill. This time several miles south of the emigrant camp.

He had difficulty accepting what a suspicion told him: They were heading back toward the emigrant camp. He calculated the time of day, calculated how much of a ride it would be for them to get back there, and shook his head.

It would be nightfall when they got back up there.

It made no sense; they had left dead comrades at that camp, had barely gotten away alive, knew how many armed emigrants were there, it just plain made no sense — unless a man speculated that this time the renegades would take hostages in darkness and offer to ransom them, something a few experienced stalkers might accomplish despite all that had happened at the emigrant camp.

He rode along their back-trail without haste, the buckskin plodded along head down, reins sagging, hungry but no longer thirsty, the hunger would have to wait, he understood; every time a two-legged creature got on his back he had to do what was required of him even if he had not been decently cared for.

They watered at another warm-water creek devoid of trout but with an abundance of skippers and mosquitoes. Farther along the buckskin's superior sense of smell made him miss a lead and raise his head, ears pointing.

Rick swung off, secured the horse and went ahead on foot. There were occasional slanting rays of sunlight, indicating that the forest was thinning.

He was familiar with the open country ahead, but actually never got close enough to see much of it because the tracks swung eastward and seemed to continue in the new direction.

He swore, hiked back, got astride and did not follow the tracks, but instead angled so as to intercept the tracks farther along.

It was a reckless thing to do. He was still vulnerable to an ambush, and for a fact the renegades knew, without seeing any indication of it, that they were hunted men; they had always been hunted after a raid.

Rick came to a trampled place where his prey had halted, perhaps to rest the livestock, but just as likely to hold a palaver.

This place also presented Rick with visible evidence that while they had stopped and he kept coming, he was closer to them than he had ever been.

The renegades' trail after they had halted continued due east. Rick followed a short distance, stopped to look for the sun's position, decided if he continued to follow the renegades he would still be behind them when they got up to the emigrant camp.

He changed course, riding back northward where no sunlight reached, and for the first time asked haste of his horse.

If he had remained at the camp — but he hadn't. Also, if he remained there he would have been caught flat-footed like everyone else back there when the renegades appeared again.

He did not like pushing the buckskin, but a lot of responsibility rode with him.

As he rode northward skirting among big trees he was convinced what the renegades had in mind was crazy, but he did not underestimate them either.

As far as he knew, that was the only wagon camp in the country, which it was, and human vultures had more than that one reason for wanting to raid it again. The alternative for the outlaws would be to abandon the idea and head out of the country with nothing to show for all their scheming and riding.

When he thought it would be safe to do so, Rick reined toward the final tier of trees. By the time he could see open country the sun was down, shadows were growing longer and darker, and although he could not see the camp he knew about where it was; north and westerly.

The buckskin seemed to sense he was on his way back; he angled down out of timber to grassy sidehill and made his descent quickly, which meant the man on his back was jolted with every step.

Rick halted once, before dusk settled, to study the southward country for sign of riders. He saw none, which he couldn't have seen if the renegades were several miles in that direction, started the horse moving again until they reached flat land, then boosted him over into an easy lope.

Half an hour later he caught sight

of firelight. Another mile closer he could see how the light bounced off wagon canvases. He was getting closer, which pleased him, tired though he was.

He slackened the pace, watched firelight get closer, and was less than a mile away when the buckskin snorted and violently shied. Before Rick got square in the saddle a man challenged him from the darkness.

"Hold it right where you are! Get off that horse!"

Rick swung to the ground.

"Who are you?"

"Rick Telly."

The man prone in the grass with a carbine snugged back and cocked, was silent for a moment before he said, "What're you doin' comin' up from the south?"

Rick recognized the voice as the other man had made the same identification. "They're comin' back."

Calvin got stiffly to his feet and eased down the carbine hammer as he gestured. "Come closer."

Rick led the buckskin up to Calvin Stuart. "What the hell," he asked, "are you doin' out here?"

"Well, Mister Calhoun got scouts out all around. He don't trust anythin' in this damned country . . . Who's comin' back?"

"The raiders."

Calvin swore. "That don't make sense. We buried four of 'em. They'd be crazy to come back."

Rick did not dispute that. He said, "Last time they got inside, Calvin. This time they got Betts as a hostage."

Calvin slung the Winchester in the crook of an arm and jerked his head. They walked side by side as Calvin related all that had been done during the day. He looked around sharply. "Are you hungry?"

Rick smiled. "As a bitch wolf, so's my horse."

When they were close Calvin called ahead as they walked. They were met just outside the wagon circle by Mike

Calhoun. He offered no greeting he simply said, "Did you find her?"

Rick shook his head. "I trailed them; as far as I could make out from the ground they only stopped once, which was when they changed course. They were riding east when I broke off to get back. I think they figure to raid the camp again."

This statement brought an identical reaction from the large man as it had brought from Calvin. "Again? They can't be more'n half the men they had before."

Rick said exactly what he had told Calvin. "But they got Betts to trade with."

Calhoun was quiet for a moment. "That won't work Mister Telly."

"They're *coyote*, Mister Calhoun. They snuck inside the last time."

The big man fell in beside Rick as the three of them walked toward a place where the barricade had been removed. He said nothing until they had climbed over the wagon tongue, where the supper fire reached them. He addressed Calvin.

"Find more men, place them out yonder. Have most of 'em southward . . . Put the fear of Gawd in 'em so's they won't fall asleep."

Calvin walked away carrying the Winchester balanced over his shoulder. Mike Calhoun watched him go and said, "He's a good man."

Rick sat on the wagon tongue, he did not have to agree or confirm that remark. He was thinking of something else.

"Ambushing those bastards don't worry me, now that we know they'll be along. What worries me is your daughter."

The large man sat on the same wagon tongue. He spoke while watching people eating at the fire. "If she gets half a chance she'll come through. Mister Telly, my daughter is tougher'n my son. It should have been the other way around, him a girl, her a boy."

Rick did not like what had been said but he was too prudent to say so. "I tried to shoot Copeland. I'd like another chance, but right now I'm hungry, thirsty and dog-tired."

The big man led Rick to the fire where the tall widow-woman handed him a heaped tin plate of hot food. He thanked her, thought briefly about her dead husband, then attacked the food. While he was eating a lanky emigrant strolled over and sat on a log beside him. He very methodically rolled and lighted a smoke before speaking.

"Didn't find her, eh?"

"No. I cut back when they turned around."

The emigrant stared, smoke trickled upwards making him squint. "That don't make sense, Mister Telly."

Rick held his cup for the tall woman to re-fill it. It was not especially good coffee, but it was hot. He explained his idea of the returning raiders to the emigrant as he had to Calvin and Calhoun. The emigrant smoked for a while before speaking.

"You ever wish you was back where you came from, Mister Telly? I almost have several times since we struck out for Oregon. Back yonder raiders hit now an' then, but they don't come back the same day . . . Where are they this time?"

"South."

"How many?"

"I didn't get close enough to count them, but if you folks killed four, there can't be more'n five or six left."

The emigrant turned grave eyes. "Why come back?"

"Maybe to trade Calhoun's daughter for money."

"They don't know Mike Calhoun."

Rick hoped the emigrant was wrong. He licked the plate clean with bread, wiped both hands down the outside legs of his britches and watched the lanky man walk away.

Calvin came to the fire to dragoon several men. As he took them away a bedraggled woman Rick remembered from being given a six-gun from inside her wagon, asked why Calvin had taken the men away.

Rick told her. She stared at him, then hastened away. He thought what he had said had probably just about unstrung the woman. Everyone had limits.

When he arose from the fire ring someone came up beside him. He looked around and smiled. It was Betts Calhoun's brother. He no longer had that odd look Rick had noticed at their last meeting.

They walked over to a wagon where Pat Calhoun asked about his sister. Rick told him what he had said before; he had not seen his sister, that he thought the returning renegades would have her with them to trade for valuables. He was wrong but that would be proven later.

Young Calhoun accepted all that with no show of emotion. "All they'll do is get killed."

Rick's reply was short. "That's fine.

I worry about your sister."

Young Calhoun nodded about that and walked away leaving Rick looking after him in a perplexed way. If he got the chance he'd like to spend a little time with the lad, who seemed somehow detached, different; it intrigued Rick.

The emigrant who had given him the six-gun approached carrying a tin cup of coffee too hot to drink. He had heard of the returning renegades and said he hoped he was nearby when they arrived. He also asked if Betts Calhoun would be with them.

Rick told him what he had surmised and the emigrant stood in silence for a moment before commenting. "Mike Calhoun'll figure hard about that. If they get all our valuables, he knows we'll have nothin' when we reach the Oregon country. No seed money to get started with."

Rick looked closely at the other man. "Calhoun's daughter's life is worth somethin' isn't it?"

The emigrant did not argue. "Yes it is, an' if she was my daughter I'd give everythin' they wanted if folks run me off afterwards. But Betts ain't my daughter an' I'm not Mike Calhoun."

Rick made a smoke, rested against the wagon, watched people, noticed that very few men were in sight, killed the smoke and went up where the livestock were. The horses had been confined inside the circle since the attack, they were tucked up enough to watch Rick's approach with hopeful eyes.

His big horses had lost considerable weight. The longer he looked at them, the longer he remembered the tired, fearful faces back down by the fire, the more cold anger he felt, and the less sleepy his body seemed to be.

He sought the emigrant who had that quiet drawl and asked if he could borrow the man's Winchester.

The emigrant handed the gun over without a word until Rick was heading toward the southern part of the circle, then he said, "I'm obliged m'buckskin horse come back no worse off than tired an' hungry . . . When you return m'gun, I'd feel pleased if it was shot empty."

11

'Too Dark'

THERE was a subtle alteration in the mood of the emigrants. They had been solemn before, after Rick's return they appeared to have little to say to each other, their bearing indicated a sense of apathy bordering on deep depression. Women showed this most, but the men who were still inside the circle did not cluster as they usually had, they tended to remain apart from each other.

Mike Calhoun approached Rick from the south, not quite as distinctly visible this night as he had been last night, the moon had passed through its quarters to the last one.

He nodded and leaned in solemn silence for a while before speaking. "They won't get inside. Not this time.

We got just about everyone out there but old men and kids."

Rick stared into the dying fire saying nothing. Calhoun looked at him. "You figure they will?"

"All I know, Mister Calhoun, that we're greenhorns an' they aren't. I want to find your daughter. I don't care what you do, or what I have to do, I just want her back safe."

The massive bearded man settled more comfortably against the wagon. "I told you, Betts is tough."

Rick turned slowly, saying nothing. The larger man shifted a little where he leaned. "We been sacrificin' since we struck out, Mister Telly. We're better'n two-thirds way to our goal, that is close enough for another sacrifice, if we got to make it."

Rick watched the large man. Reading a face covered with a beard was impossible. He returned his gaze to the fire ring.

Calhoun spoke again. "I'll get her back," he said quietly. "If I can. You aren't one of us so most likely that don't sound right to you."

Rick straightened up to depart. He wasn't sure he felt the same way toward Mike Calhoun he had felt before this crisis had arrived. Calhoun said, "Wait."

Rick waited.

"You've been a real help to us. We appreciate it, believe me. You'll get your horses back; I'll give the money back to the folks who bought them in good faith. I got a feelin' about you'n my daughter. I don't disapprove. But right now where we're camped tonight, seems to me to be the turnin' point of all we've sweated and slaved for."

Rick softly said, "Mister Calhoun, if Betts was my daughter I'd let 'em kill me before I'd leave her to those wolves."

"Mister Telly, that's exactly what I aim to do. I'm goin' to get my daughter back from that scum if they kill me for trying. If they show up here with her, I got to get between her an' them — kill or get killed."

Rick released a long, slow breath. They looked at each other for a moment, then Rick walked away. Mike Calhoun watched him depart. He'd had one more thing to say. He had wanted to ask Rick to stand beside him when the moment came.

An old man appeared out of darkness acting agitated but deferential. He said, "Mister Calhoun, they'd like to see you at your wagon."

The large man saw the older man's anxiety. "What is it, Amos?"

"Mister Calhoun, there's one of them fellers at your wagon."

Calhoun straightened up slowly, walked past the old man looking at the eerily moonlighted wagon near the southwesterly curve of the wagon circle.

When he got down there another emigrant was standing with a rifle in the crook of his arm. He said, "Inside. How he got past the fellers out yonder

I don't know. He just come over the wagon tongue and tapped old Amos on the shoulder. There's three of us around the wagon. You give the word an' we'll hang the son of a bitch from that upraised wagon tongue."

Calhoun climbed into the wagon. The renegade was a dirty, unkempt man with a narrow face, a long jaw and close-set grey eyes. He was sitting on a trunk carving off a chew when Calhoun climbed in. The renegade had lighted a candle. The light was adequate because canvas stretched over ash bows reflected light. He closed his knife, pocketed it, cheeked the tobacco and nodded. "My name is Marty Fisher, wagon master. I'll tell you why I'm here. We got your girl an' we'll slit her throat unless you round all them clod hoppers up and get 'em to fetch their money an' valuables to this wagon . . . Mister wagon master, don't even think about goin' for that gun. One gunshot an' her throat gets slashed."

Mike Calhoun went to a pile of bedding and sat down. He had been certain the moment for something like this would arrive. He had rather thought that the renegades would call their demands from beyond where emigrants were lying in wait out yonder. What Rick Telly had said was evidently true, these men were very experienced.

The watching renegade spoke quietly. "I understand you're between hell an' high water, but they ain't goin' to wait all night for me to come back."

Mike Calhoun studied the renegade closely. The man was one of those lined, weathered individuals who could be almost any age. He wore his gun tied to one leg, the grip was worn-smooth walnut darkened by sweat. Anywhere Calhoun might have encountered Marty Fisher, he would have avoided him.

"I can ask," Calhoun said. "That's all I can do. Folks don't part with seed money, Mister Fisher. Not without one hell of a reason."

"Well now, wagon master, you tell one of them lads outside to tell your emigrants what they got to do to get the lady back. You let 'em know what'll happen if they hang fire."

Calhoun did not move. "I can give you what I have."

Fisher sneered. "How much is that?"

"Three thousand dollars in gold."

Fisher looked surprised, but that passed. "Maybe the others got that much too. We got to have it all — or Aaron's goin' to slash her throat an' leave her where you folks can find her. Aaron's real handy with a knife; when you find her, wagon master, her head'll be hangin' by a thread from her body." Marty Fisher chewed for a moment before also saying. "Aaron's took a real shine to your daughter. He might put off cuttin' her throat until they've been right friendly a time or two."

The large man's hands slowly clenched and unclenched. "I'll talk to the fellers outside." As Calhoun was arising he added a little more. "Like I said, Mister

Fisher, all I can do is ask."

The renegade nodded, watched the large man pass beyond the front canvas, heard him repeating the raider's demand or they would kill his daughter, and was about ready to jettison his cud when Calhoun returned, sat down gazing at the outlaw from his unreadable face.

Fisher gave his ultimatum. "Half hour, wagon master."

Calhoun shook his head slowly. "It'll take longer'n that to convince folks they got to part with everythin' they've saved and hoarded, Mister Fisher. We're not talkin' about buyin' or sellin' horses, we're talkin' about the future of a wagon train."

The renegade's close-set grey eyes were fixed on Mike Calhoun. He almost smiled. "While we're wastin' time I can tell you I wasn't the only one figured you'd have scouts. Couple friends of mine also come in real close, just in case someone needs killin' while you'n me are palavering."

Calhoun did not appear very impressed. "If Aaron's one of them, no matter what happens he'll never leave this place."

The sound of Marty Fisher's laughter masked a faintly abrasive sound of someone listening outside the wagon as Fisher spoke again.

"It ain't Aaron, wagon master. He's got two busted ribs. He had a hell of a time makin' the ride we made to get back here without whoever was trackin' us close. Aaron's back yonder with the woman. He couldn't make it the last couple miles."

Calhoun thought he heard leather grind faintly over earth and spoke quickly. "How about horses? We could trade you livestock for — ."

"Horses," snorted the renegade. "We get horses every time we pass a town or a big ranch."

Calhoun allowed silence to settle. The renegade sliced off a sliver of his tobacco and, using the dull side of the knife raised it to his mouth.

His eyes did not leave Calhoun even after he had the tobacco in his mouth. He offered Calhoun the knife and plug. Calhoun shook his head. As Fisher was pocketing his plug and clasp knife he said, "It beats hell out of being hungry, wagon master . . . How long is it goin' to take them damned clod hoppers to hand over their goods? Like I said, I don't have all night, and the fellers with me said you had no more'n half an hour after I give you our terms."

Calhoun shrugged. "I told you — gettin' folks to hand everything over will take time. What you're askin' is for them to arrive in Oregon with nothin' but their livestock an' wagons. It'll be a real hard choice. They been lookin' forward to takin' up farms ever since we started out, they've gone through a lot to get this far."

"Not if they like your daughter, wagon master. Not if they don't want to see a pretty woman with her head half off. They'll give, or we'll wait farther along, catch the lot of you asleep some night, an' set fire to everything you got. Wagon master, you'n your clod hoppers got us real mad today. Real mad. We got to have revenge. You shot Wayne Begley. He's been our leader for two years an' was a real good man."

Calhoun waited for silence then asked if Fisher would like a drink during their wait. The outlaw sneered. "No thanks. I don't drink whiskey with no clod hoppers — or sheepmen . . . That three thousand in gold: You got it hid in here somewhere?"

Before Calhoun could reply one of the men outside called to him. Instantly, the renegade's six-gun came out and upwards. "Set where you are," he said, then raised his voice. "What d'you want?"

A drawling voice that sounded almost impersonal answered. "Some folks want to talk."

"Talk? Mister, you got about ten minutes. There's nothin' to talk about."

The drawling voice said, "They want to know how much you'll settle for?"

This time the renegade's six-gun swiveled toward the front of the wagon where that drawling, almost taunting voice came from. "All of it, clod hopper. Every dollar an' whatever jewelry like gold rings you got." His voice had been raised, but even if he had been talking in his normal range he would have been unable to hear the knife that cut the pucker string holding the rear canvas above the tailgate.

Calhoun, who was facing the renegade saw hands silently part the canvas, saw guns appear over the tailgate where men's heads and shoulders appeared. He caught his breath.

Fisher called one more time. "You sons of bitches, ten more minutes!"

Fisher was leaning a little watching the front where the seat was, his six-gun stone-steady. He seemed to expect some argument from out front.

No one up there made a sound, but from the opposite end of the wagon a sharp, hard voice spoke with unmistakable menace.

"*Put the gun down.*"

Fisher stiffened without moving. He knew better than to look around, to make any abrupt movement. He did not lower the gun; he looked at Mike Calhoun as though to speak when that other voice spoke again, quietly but with the same menacing sound. "*Put it down!*"

Fisher had a hostage in front of him, a large one he could not miss. Several guns were cocked behind him. He put the six-gun down, looked venomously at Mike Calhoun but remained silent.

The wagon master noticeably sagged. He had just survived the most deadly situation he could ever encounter.

A large emigrant came in from the front with a cocked pistol. Behind him another emigrant crowded close. From the tailgate that drawling voice said. "Well, I don't mind bein' wrong once in a while. We got the son of a bitch."

The man looking in from out front gestured to Marty Fisher, "Stand up.

Now then, come toward me. Keep both hands in front . . . Mister Calhoun, get his gun."

They climbed down out front where the night was turning chilly. Marty Fisher looked at them. There were six emigrants, not a one of which showed so much as a glimmer of mercy.

For moments they exchanged stares. Fisher faced the situation he had been progressing toward all of his forty-one years. Whatever else he was, Marty Fisher was not a coward. He spat and spoke to Mike Calhoun. "There's others yonder. You walk me out where they can see an' they'll cut you to pieces."

The lanky, drawling man with sunk-set grey eyes leaned on his rifle eyeing Fisher. He shifted a cud from one cheek to the other before saying, "Mister . . . There ain't nobody out there. Turn around."

Fisher turned. As he stared out where the upraised wagon tongue was skylined he saw his companions standing among emigrant men with arms bound behind their backs.

One of the emigrants from out there softly called. "You get him?"

The drawling man called back in the same seemingly detached tone. "We got him. Calvin? You ready?"

"Ready as we'll ever be. Bring the son of a bitch along. He can go first."

They were hard men. Each renegade had seen death and dying many times. They had been callous at those times and they were callous now. If the emigrants expected any of them to beg or whine, they were disappointed. Just one renegade even spoke, and he cursed the emigrants, told them none would die in bed, said where they were going if Indians didn't torture their women and children, other renegades would. It was a chilling statement.

Mike Calhoun raised a hand as the other emigrants placed the speaker directly beneath the upraised wagon tongue. He asked where his daughter was.

The renegade sneered, ignored Calhoun and growled at the nearest emigrant. "Get the gawddamned rope in place, you ugly, ignorant son of a bitch."

This man was like lead, but every hand on the rope had a willing heart behind it. Before they could tie the rope back the dangling man kicked, convulsed, twisted and turned, motions which made handling the rope more difficult, but they got the rope around a spoke, took up slack and tied it fast, then stood watching the renegade strangle to death.

It required time to hang a man, wait for him to strain his last, lower him, drag the carcass clear and position the next man. The night was getting colder as it wore along toward dawn.

The hangings were accomplished in near darkness, the full moon which had been up there several nights in a row, was now slower arising and with each passing night had a part of it missing.

There were watchers, faint shadows

back among the wagons. It wasn't seemly for a woman to watch lynchings, but exceptions were emigrant women who had lost their men, or had patched wounds.

Farther off, up where cooking fires were never allowed to die completely, there was a reddish glow that barely reached out where the second renegade went through his dying restrictions, legs treading air, body arching high and twisting.

Mike Calhoun sought Calvin Stuart, whose face reflected flickering red firelight, and asked where Rick Telly was.

Without lowering his eyes from what was to him a sight to relish and remember as that man strangling aloft struggled, Calvin spoke offhandedly while looking upwards. "He left on a borrowed horse half hour 'go, ridin' south. I helped him rig out. He'd got close to the wagon you'n that fish-eyed bastard up there was talkin' in. He come after me to help him get a horse.

I did. All he said was that he figured he knew about where Betts was, and rode off. I loaned him my Winchester . . . Well, that one's limp." Calvin lowered his head. "You don't expect us to bury that carrion do you?"

Calhoun walked away without replying and Calvin went forward to help get enough slack so others could work the bowline knot loose and let the dead man down.

A lanky man stood with a youth gazing dispassionately at the lined-up corpses. "Somethin' you might want to remember, Patrick. There's good an' bad in most men. Then again, there's some born with only bad in them, an' while it's not a pleasant sight lookin' at them like we're doin' right now, they got to be socked away. A Mormon friend of mine called it 'sending them to hell across lots', which I never understood but there they are. They come through a lot of years bringin' misery to decent folks, and here they're goin' to stay. It's got precious little to do with written law lad, but it's got everythin' to do with justice . . . Come along, let's go find some hot coffee."

Young Calhoun looked at the older man. "Do we look up now and nod?"

The older man smiled. "All right, let's do it."

They looked into the faintly paling overhead and nodded. When they finished Pat Calhoun said, "I didn't see anyone nod back."

The older man said, "Too dark. Let's get that coffee."

12

No Time for Fear

THIS time Rick's borrowed horse was rangy, black and with somewhat a mind of his own. Rick did not know, hadn't asked and in fact hadn't cared, but the rawboned big black horse, who could probably run a hole in the daylight, belonged to a man who was unique among emigrants, he knew horses, for which reason he never castrated until they were three years old and had bred a few mares. It allowed a horse's neck to develop, get a stud-horse bow to it.

It also took time for new geldings to forget horsing mares, eventually they would. The black horse was nine years old. Mares no longer interested him, but during his rutting time he had developed an independent turn of mind which he would never lose.

For example, when Rick eased him over into a lope, because he was tall, rangy and strong, he decided to run and it took better than a mile for Rick to haul him down, start over, and do this four times before the black horse decided to obey, to shorten his gait to an easy lope.

It probably did not help that there was a pre-dawn chill in the morning; animals, particularly horses, were high-headed first thing on a chilly morning.

Rick rode by hope and prayer because he did not know where the renegades had reached low country to turn north. He *did* know that if Aaron Copeland heard him, he would be waiting in ambush.

But with dew on the grass, and also because Rick was riding a barefoot horse, he did not make much noise.

If it had been daylight he could have backtracked, but from the look of the eastern sky daylight would be a while yet.

Once he halted and looked back. For some reason he did not try to pin down, he had a feeling there was a rider behind him. Maybe more than one rider. But whoever it was had to be some distance back because he could neither hear nor see anyone.

The black horse did an inexcusable thing under the circumstances, normal though it was. He heartily blew his nose.

Rick could have brained him. In the utter silence of pre-dawn that sound would carry one hell of a distance. Rick had a hunch Aaron was not far ahead.

A light ankle-high wind brisked up from the south. It bent tall grass heads and rattled old dry leaves but otherwise, because it passed northward in a hurry, the sensation of cold air passed quickly.

Rick swung off and led the horse. He quartered back and forth, found no tracks of riders going north, wondered with a sinking heart if he had come too far south, but instead of turning back to quarter, he continued southward.

It required time to sashay back and forth pretty close to a half mile on each hike east and west, mostly east because westerly, as soon as the ground began to tilt toward the highlands, he turned to angle southwesterly again.

The black horse followed on a slack rein like a puppy. Without the faintest idea of what they were doing, he did it anyway; someone had worked him well on the ground. He followed the slightest tug on the rein. He also stood without moving when mounted, something riders could appreciate as opposed to those annoying horses who took a forward step or two as soon as they felt a boot in a stirrup.

The chill increased as did the deep, enduring stillness. Rick paused often with his head cocked. He did not expect to hear Aaron, but there were two saddle animals with Copeland and his captive. Horses, even the laziest, most dully phlegmatic of them, got bored from standing and shifted around now and then. Hungry or thirsty horses were the worst, they became restless and agitated.

But Rick heard nothing. He was on one of his easterly sashays when he found tracks. The renegades had ridden down out of the uplands much farther south than he had expected.

He knelt to be reassured. There were distinct shod-horse tracks. What he could not tell in darkness was how many riders there had been.

He arose and started west, pausing now and then to lean for reassurance he was on the right track.

He was. In that country riders were rare. Farther south and on both sides of Crested Butte there were cattle outfits. Where he was tracking there hadn't been cattle this close to the mountains in years; there were too many bears and lions whose vantage points among the big trees high up, would allow the meat-eaters to lay careful traps, and if they missed ambushing a critter, both of them were capable of running them down. Cougars were very fast, bears too, although only people who had never seen a top-heavy pigeon-toed bear run would believe it. An old sow-bear with hungry cubs could out-run some horses. The only cattle she would have trouble with were razor-backed longhorns who had many times out-run very fast horses. And too, longhorns would fight; with a horn-spread of anywhere from four to six feet, longhorns could and often did impale a bear. But longhorns were no longer the critter of choice among beef stockmen.

With no other tracks, Rick did not follow them easterly beyond the point where they turned north in the direction of the emigrant camp, he found a spindly pine tree, left the black horse, took the Winchester and quartered to find where two horses had branched off.

Dawn was breaking before he found the place. He might never have found it if watery-grey light had not brightened his world a little.

Two horses had broken away from the other tracks not very far down the slope. He worried that Aaron would be able to see him as daylight strengthened, so he hiked up the hill with burning lungs in order to reach timber before sunrise. Up there, he sat down to catch his breath and await daylight. From higher up he hoped to be able to see where Copeland's two horses were hobbled or tied. He did not expect to see either Betts or her captor unless they moved, which he did not expect them to do, Copeland particularly with broken ribs and worn to a frazzle from lack of sleep.

He got the surprise of his life when something stepped on dead twigs behind him. It was not a varmint; it had to be something large and heavy. He twisted with the Winchester on the rise.

A majestic buck mule deer was back a short distance clearly as astonished to see the man move as Rick was to see the big animal. He still had a swollen neck although rutting season was past. The buck was large, fleshed out, as beautiful a deer as Rick would ever see. But right at the moment of their unexpected confrontation, he only noticed the thick neck. Male deer, timid any other time of the year, would fight anything, including a buzz saw, when they were in the rut.

Rick's heart thudded in its dark place. If he had to kill the buck the sound of his gunshot would carry for miles. He sweated despite the chill, breathed shallowly and waited.

The buck ducked his head a couple of times, which could mean either he meant to intimidate the two-legged thing or that he intended to charge.

He did not paw, fling dirt over his back and rock back the way fighting deer did just before charging.

Rick spoke quietly without expecting it to have any effect, but he felt better doing it. "I don't want to kill you. Just turn and walk away. Go on, walk off."

The buck rattled his horns at the sound of the man's voice, made a couple more lowering gestures of warning, stamped hard with one foot, turned and did not run. He walked northward into the trees taking very high, jerky steps while watching the two-legged creature with his head cocked slightly to one side.

Rick lowered the Winchester. His body loosened, his heart began to slacken its beat, the big buck finally passed among the trees and disappeared.

Rick mopped off sweat with a sleeve, wished mightily for a smoke, settled for a chew, and let a minute or two pass before easing behind a huge fir tree where he could see the downslope and most of the country beyond.

There was no movement, no dozing horses, only a jumble of prehistoric rocks. Rick straightened up very slowly; hell, that was the same boulder field he had watched Copeland and Curlew disappear into.

His earlier tracking had been mostly in darkness. He had not placed the immense rocks in relation to the rearward uplands.

He sank to one knee, leaned on the Winchester, and concentrated on the boulder field. The distance was considerable, the grass was tall, but he made out where two large animals had made a path directly in among the boulders, most of whom were as tall as a mounted man, and with a few exceptions, the others were nearly that tall.

There was no sense of exaltation, only one of anticipation tinged with dread about Betts Calhoun.

He was sure they were hiding down there, but except for the thin trail leading among the boulders, he had nothing else to bolster his feeling. What he searched vainly for was horses, but they could be down there and even from his high ground, he would be unable to see them if they were among the large rocks.

His second cause for anxiety was now that the sun was rising, how he could get down there without being seen, even if he belly-crawled the entire distance.

It was too late to employ the darkness which had been a hindrance and which would now be a blessing.

He thought about calling to Copeland to come out, to put down his weapons, but that thought left almost as quickly as it had arrived. Injured, certain to be found sooner or later if he could not leave the rocks, Copeland only had one ace in his hand: Betts Calhoun.

Rick got restlessly to his feet, moved deeper into the forest and skirted southward until he thought he might be far enough along for a better view inside the rock field. He still saw nothing, livestock or human, and now he could no longer make out the trail of two horses.

The sun was climbing with inexorable

slowness but there was daylight, the entire world shone brilliantly under an azure sky.

Rick leaned, got rid of his cud, studied the rocks from every angle. There was no way anyone could approach them without being seen providing someone was watching and sure as hell Copeland would be watching. He was probably chomping at the bit for sight of his companions returning. By just about any measurement of time they should have shown up by now.

Rick knelt, tipped his hat, narrowed his eyes and very slowly and methodically ran his glance along the northernmost boulders which would be the direction Copeland would be watching. If he could see northward he had to be doing it over the top of a boulder, which was what Rick concentrated on finding; something like a man's hat and shoulders among the boulders. If the man moved it would help, but there was no movement and as closely as he could tell, there was no man.

But there was a very distant small band of horsemen. Their movement was easily discernible. They were back-tracking the earlier renegades, but to Rick, and to the fugitive among the rocks, it seemed more like returning outlaws. Only Rick knew this could not be.

Those distant horsemen had to be emigrants back-tracking Copeland's companions. Rick hunkered and watched. They would never find the sidehill tracks where Copeland had branched off because they were riding arrow-straight southward.

But they stopped where tracks came down the sidehill, sat briefly talking and looking up there. Rick would have bet his life they would not go up the hill and he would have won; they didn't, they sat out there talking and gesturing. They had come to the end of the north-bound tracks. All they knew that would be accomplished by climbing that slope and tracking through the timber, would be back-tracking the renegades northward to where they had come up into the highlands from their failed attack on the wagons. Full circle. That was not what bearded big Mike Calhoun and the slitty-eyed older man beside him were down here for. They knew Aaron had not arrived at the wagon camp with Betts. They knew he was still alive. What they did not know was — where he was. Their foremost worry was Betts Calhoun. Copeland they would take care of below the nearest tree, Betts Calhoun they hoped in every man's heart, would be unharmed when they found her.

Rick turned from watching the distant horsemen. Among the rocks there was nothing visible. He was fishing for his tobacco when the glass-still air carried a faint sound of something scraping over brittle talus or scree.

The sound had come from the boulder field. Rick forgot about the tobacco, leaned to hear more. But there was no additional sound, and even what he had heard had been so faint he was almost prepared to believe he had heard nothing.

A commotion back yonder dragged his attention away from the rocks very briefly. Someone had found the tethered black horse. Now, the grouped emigrants got to the ground talking and gesturing. One lanky man with a rifle and a prominent Adam's-apple walked away from the others, walked as far as the lift of westward country, stood looking up there a long time before returning to his companions to tell them someone, and he'd bet new money he knew who it was, had left tracks from where the black horse had been tied, and had climbed straight up that damned sidehill.

Rick returned his stare to the rocks. He needed a miracle, otherwise he was going to have to hide up there until dusk, which he did not want to do. He was not just anxious to rescue Calhoun's daughter, he was also spitting cotton, his stomach thought his throat had been cut, and his eyes felt like there were grains of sand beneath the lids.

Whatever was done he had to accomplish soon.

It probably wasn't a miracle, it was possibly more like a simple, pragmatic undertaking by very earthy, practical men, but in either event the emigrants got back astride with one man trailing the black horse, and continued riding southward.

Whatever their reason for doing this was, Rick had no idea. They had already seen where the renegades had come down to flat ground from the uplands. They knew their tracks went northward toward the wagon camp, and the direction in which they were now riding, southward past a boulder field on their right, there were no tracks, no sign of anything except perhaps some small game.

In fact, what they had decided was that somewhere along the way they might find two sets of horse tracks, so continuing to go southward might eventually bring them to the sign they sought. There was nothing wrong with their logic; if Copeland and his prisoner had not been among the outlaws at the wagon camp, then they had probably trailed southward up in the timber until eventually coming down to flat ground. There was nothing wrong with their logic, it just wasn't correct.

Rick watched the emigrants. The distance was not so great he could not make out the unmistakable bulk of the bearded man on the twelve-hundred pound horse.

He lowered his gaze to the rocks. He knew as well as he knew his name that Copeland was watching, only now in order to see the emigrants pass easterly, he would have to turn his back on the uplands with their fringe of forest giants.

Rick spat, rubbed a bristly jaw, lifted and re-set his hat, estimated when the emigrants would pass below the rocks, and moved in behind the largest tree after which there were no more, just that tall-grass downslope leading toward the rocks.

It was a considerable distance. If he got too far from the trees to run back while also being too far from the boulders to use them for protection, *if* Copeland looked back, Rick was very likely to get killed — providing Copeland had the usual hard-rider's saddle gun, whose range would out-distance any handgun ever made. In fact if Copeland had a carbine and Rick had his rifle, the fateful few seconds it would take for both to aim, would be in Copeland's favour.

He left the timber to start the descent. He wanted to run, but that would surely make noise. He walked carefully, avoiding loose rocks, alternately watched his footing and the huge rocks on the west side of the boulder field.

If he could get downslope far enough he could keep the big rocks between himself and the place where Copeland was.

Normally a man in his situation, if he had the sense Gawd gave a goose, would be very much afraid, but when the same man had a firm goal in mind, along with a powerful need to kill another man, and get safely close enough to do it, he had no time for fear.

If the man survived the fear would come later when every nerve under his hide would start crawling.

13

Rick's Mistake

THE emigrants with the large bearded man out front rode at a walk. Rick only peripherally watched them. His life depended on getting close enough to the field of huge boulders to be protected from discovery. He no longer made an attempt to see the people amid the boulders.

The emigrants prolonged the anxiety by halting roughly parallel to the field of boulders. While they sat talking Rick continued to advance until he had tall, massive rocks between himself and the people ahead. For the first time since leaving the uplands, Rick felt safe; at least he had less to fear from the renegade he was stalking, although that might not last long. It depended on the emigrants a dozen or so yards eastward of the boulders.

Rick could faintly hear voices, words were indistinguishable but he was satisfied it had to be the emigrants sitting out there like ducks on a pond, completely vulnerable without knowing it.

He covered the last hundred or so yards, leaned against cool stone, rested briefly before edging toward the north edge of the big rock. Those distant voices were still barely audible. He thought Aaron Copeland, being closer, would be able to hear what was being said. Rick spared only a moment to reflect; his guess was that the emigrants were arguing, one contending that continuing southward would be a waste of time, the others, perhaps with Betts Calhoun's father among them, pointing out that since they had not found evidence that Copeland had come down from the timbered uplands, he had to either be still up there, or had possibly ridden southward while still up there, before coming down to open country.

However this might have ended, a pack of frightened coyotes, a dog, a bitch and four youngsters, came out of the boulder field where they must have been lying in terrified seclusion, probably in a den, running as fast as they could, not sounding which coyotes commonly did, but concentrating on getting out of the area as fast as they could.

Rick did not see them but he heard a man shout among the emigrants. No one made any outcry after that one startled yell.

Rick had been able to make out the word 'coyotes' but that was all. He used what he hoped would be a distraction to peek around the edge of his big rock. All he saw was more rocks, large, very large and small. He compounded his risk by hovering longer than prudence suggested; long enough to see a way into the boulder field. He moved in jerks and starts going from rock to rock.

The emigrants were moving again, southward. Rick finally had them in full view. So did Aaron Copeland whose relief must have been great as the only peril he was aware of rode slowly southward.

Rick heard a noise close by and dropped flat. By leaving his hat on the ground and inching around his protective rock he saw something that made him feel vindicated but otherwise not much better. Two hobbled horses, rolling small rocks with their noses in search of something to eat, of which there was very little.

Copeland was not in sight. Rick took risks trying to locate him. Nor did he see Betts Calhoun, but they were close by, somewhere. Those horses had not hobbled themselves.

For the time being he did not look for the woman. Copeland had to be among the onward rocks watching the emigrants. Rick was much farther back. Between them were tumbled rocks of all sizes. There was barely room enough for a man to put his feet without touching a rock, but most frustrating for the manhunter was the irregular wall of those mounted-man-high upright rocks which formed a backdrop for the foremost barricade of rocks where someone would have to be in order to see open country — and departing emigrants.

He felt heat but the rocks were still cool, and would remain cool until mid-afternoon. He began belly-crawling, had made only a little progress when he felt his shirt being shredded by sharp edge loose rock which was everywhere.

He hauled up with his back to a big boulder, dusted off where the shirt was worn through, shook his head, got down and began crawling again. The second time he nestled close to protective granite when a very distinct voice said, "As long as they're southward, you are cut off."

The retort was venomous. "Oh no, lady. We can go north with the big rocks between us an' them."

The woman's reply was curt. "North-ward, Aaron?"

"Only until we're far enough, then we can ride back up the slope an' get into the timber."

This time the reply came in a voice as dry as cold corn husks. "Be sensible. You barely made it down here. You'd never last that long. You keep going on stamina, nothing else. Stamina has its limits. Aaron you can't get away. They'll come back, they'll see us or find our tracks . . . Give up, Aaron."

"Hand me that bottle and shut up!"

Rick waited but the silence settled. He knew approximately where they were, toward the southerly perimeter of the rock field, down where there were mostly high, thick plinths of ageless granite.

He shook sweat off his face, aimed for the nearest boulder, this one in the shape of an egg but quite tall.

He made it, paused to suck air, decided to abandon his Winchester; he was close enough now to kill with a handgun. The woman's voice came again. Rick wondered if she thought nagging the renegade would help her. Rick thought otherwise, particularly if Copeland had a bottle of whiskey. Betts probably did not know it but she was taunting a man who killed without compunction. Probably the only thing that had kept her alive this long was that she was attractive. Outlaws commonly lived through long dry spells. Copeland had, beginning with when he had joined the wagon train, and during that time he had wanted Betts Calhoun. Once, he had nearly succeeded.

Rick listened as she said, "That bandage needs tightening."

The reply was harsh. "I'll make it. Busted ribs never killed anyone."

"It will ease the pain. Lean down and let me tighten it."

This time the man's voice was surly but not particularly harsh. "Jeezus Chris' woman, that's too tight."

"No it isn't. Stand back now and take a breath. Isn't that better?"

Copeland did not answer the question, he spoke on a different subject. "Betts, if they keep goin' south they won't get back here before sundown. We can make it back into the timber."

She replied quietly. "No we can't. Look . . . "

Copeland began to swear. "Damned clod hoppers. Comin' back. Well, this time they'll ride past headin' for their camp, their lousy food and poisonous coffee. We'll let 'em get far ahead. We got all the time in the world to let it get dark so's we can get back up yonder."

"The horses are in bad shape, Aaron."

He exploded. "You keep peckin' at me an' I'll leave you in these gawddamned rocks with your throat cut. I owe you, an' you know it. I never paid you back for hittin' me. You figured I'd forgot, didn't you? You stupid damned female, a man don't never forget bein' hit by a woman. Now just shut up!"

She didn't. "Aaron — ."

Rick heard the blow land and flinched, began crawling again, this time concentrating only on getting close enough. He used restraint only when he rattled stone and Copeland abruptly said, "Someone's close. One of them son of a bitching clod hoppers snuck back while we was talking . . . Betts; you're not goin' to see tomorrow's sunup. I wish to Chris' I'd never seen you. If you make a sound I'll come back and kill you. Understand? Any noise at all."

Rick looked frantically for protection, furious with himself. From being hunter he was now the hunted. He crawled with care not to be noisy about it, reached safety behind a rock and took down several deep breaths, waited, lifted out the six-gun and held it against the rock.

Any renegade who had lived as long as Aaron Copeland had, did not accomplish this by error of luck. It only occurred to Rick Telly when he had been waiting for a long time, that while his rock offered protection in front, nothing protected him from the rear. If Copeland had remained invisible and silent for so long, he was not coming directly forward. Rick twisted to look back. There was nothing to be seen or heard in that direction. Copeland was clever at stalking, that was how he had successfully made his living for years.

What Rick needed, and quickly, was a place of concealment with rocks on all sides.

There were several such places in the rock field, but none of them were close.

He strained backward again, then squinted among the westward rocks, finally he swung to seek movement on the eastward side of his rock. Nothing. No sighting, not a sound, but the son of a bitch was out there somewhere.

Rick had no time to understand how desperate his position had become. He only had time to find Copeland before he, himself, was found. He very carefully crawled twenty feet where two rocks faced each other, got between them and paused to use a filthy sleeve to push sweat away from his eyes.

Now, he had protection in front as well as behind, but no protection on either side. The improvement was slight; Aaron Copeland was still searching. He remembered what someone had said about the renegade's deadliness with a handgun, his lightning-like draw and unerring accuracy. Rick knew guns, had been around them, had handled them all his life, but his trade was cow ranching, that was what he knew best and was most experienced at. He had no illusions; in a shoot-out he was probably no match for the renegade.

He had not manoeuvred since beginning his hunt for Betts Calhoun, for a head-on confrontation with a man who was several times over better with a handgun. He did not marvel at how quickly the fates had lined up against him. He lay perfectly still, watching and listening. He had a thumb pad resting on the gnarled hammer of his weapon. If Copeland found him first . . .

Whatever happened now — whenever it happened — would be over and done with in seconds. Every sense was sharpened, his vision was acute, his hearing was better than it had ever been. He was no longer conscious of being thirsty or hungry or tired to the bone. Every instinct was at its apex of alertness.

The silence, the sun passing on a slanting angle overhead, the tension from waiting, everything in his world was keyed to the next minute, at the most the next ten minutes.

When an alien sound arrived he heard it in every detail without being diverted by it. Two round rocks rolled together. The sound had come from the west, out near that secondary irregular stand of plinths.

He faced in that direction bringing his six-gun up. What happened next was never afterwards clear. He heard a gunshot, always remembered hearing the gunshot, but when the lead slug shattered against the rock in front of him northward, everything froze in a frame of pain. He knew he was bleeding. There were actually three gunshots.

One shot seemed to come from the east where those rocks had rolled together, it had come from the opposite direction moments before he swung quickly facing the noise of rocks striking.

Movement revealed his whereabouts. He did not hear the second shot as he was punched forward, lost his gun and felt no pain when his face was torn by a sharp stone.

The second shot had been fired from the hip. It had been accurate enough to break loose a large piece of granite but not the crouching man beside the granite. The torn-loose rock struck Rick squarely between the eyes with considerable force.

The racket made by gunshots easily

reached those distant emigrants. They turned and started back in a lope. The man leading Rick's borrowed horse could not keep up with the black horse hanging back, so he let the rope drop.

The black horse who led so well, knew which way the emigrants were taking him; back to the camp where he would have food and water. The moment the rider leading him turned to go back southward, the black horse got balky. So balky that the emigrant cast off the lead rope. Without even glancing southward where the emigrants were riding, the black horse turned back northward in the direction of camp, and walked steadily along carrying his head slightly to one side in order to avoid stepping on the lead shank.

Mike Calhoun un-shipped his booted carbine as he rode, eyes fixed on the boulder field. That was the only place those gunshots could have come from.

Neither Calhoun or the men with him used caution. They'd been through enough; they would be cautious some other time.

The period of time between the second and third shots had not been long, but it had been longer than a man would require to re-cock and fire a single action six-gun.

As the riders swept close they fanned out, each one riding with a handgun up and ready. Men a-horseback riding fast made difficult targets; riders fanning out until there was at least two or three hundred feet between them, made the chance of hitting more than one rider before being overwhelmed even among rocks, very unlikely.

They did not slacken until they could no longer ride fast because of the strewn boulders, which was where they piled off, left the horses and got among the nearest rocks on the north side of the rocky area.

Calvin yelled. "Copeland, you son of a bitch, stand up and fight."

The last echo died. Mike leaned toward Calvin Stuart and stated his dread. "If he shot her I'm goin' to drag him back behind my horse."

Another emigrant sang out, this one had a drawling voice that seemed to lack any excitement. He sounded as though he were carrying on a loud conversation. He said, "Tell you what, you cornered rat, let the lady come over to us an' we'll let you stay alive . . . It's hot out here, so don't put off lettin' us see her comin' too long . . . Aaron, that's all you got. Your life for turnin' her loose."

This time a voice called from among the boulders. It was recognised instantly. "Help me. Paw, come help me."

Calvin caught the large man's sleeve as Calhoun stood up in plain sight and started forward. Calvin's caution was reasonable; the reason it didn't work was because he could no more have held back the large man than he could have restrained a bull.

Calvin and the other emigrants arose to watch, guns ready. Someone

243

muttered that Calhoun was going to get himself killed, that while it had indeed been Betts Calhoun who had called, that bastard Copeland probably had a knife at her throat.

They stood out there in the lowering afternoon brilliance neither moving nor making a sound. They no longer had Mike Calhoun in sight. But they recognised his bull-bass roar when he yelled to them. "Fetch a canteen. Whiskey too if anyone's got it . . . Calvin, gawddammit, come on, it's all over. *Come on!*"

They surged ahead, stumbling, swearing and hurrying. That lanky emigrant with the prominent Adam's apple brought the canteen.

Mike Calhoun rose out of some big rocks looking as grim as death. As he held out his hand for the canteen the emigrants crowded up as close as they could to a narrow place between two tail rocks. There was blood on Betts Calhoun's dress, hands and arms. An emigrant blurted out that she had been shot. Her father, who was wedged between the rocks turned his head. "Not *her*, you idiot, *him*!"

The emigrant retorted with spirit. "If you'd get your damned pile of mutton out'n the way so a man can see in there . . . Is it Aaron?"

"No, it's Telly," replied the large man, making no move to shift so the others could see into the narrow space.

Calvin leaned and touched Betts's shoulder. "You ain't shot?"

She spared a moment to look up from her attempt to staunch the bleeding. "I'm fine, Mister Stuart. Rick is bleeding like a stuck hawg. Any of you have clean bandanas?"

Several were offered which she took and leaned forward until her father's bulk interfered then she snapped at him. "If you want to help, Paw, figure out some way to get him back to camp."

The lanky emigrant with the prominent Adam's apple was leaning on his rifle looking around. He sounded almost plaintive when he said, "Where's Aaron?"

No one answered although other emigrants peered among the rocks.

246

14

A New Spring

SCARCELY a word was said on the ride back to the wagons. They had cobbled together a makeshift sling of bedrolls with Rick atop it and three riders on each side holding it. At best it was a crude litter, but the alternative was worse.

The lanky man with the Adam's apple brought up the rear, rifle balanced across his lap, a corpse swaying behind his cantle. He was fortunate, not every horse would stand for something leaking blood and smelling to high heaven being lashed behind the saddle.

Betts rode the horse she had been astride during her entire nightmare. She was haggard, bedraggled and dull-eyed. Her right cheek was swollen. There was a slight flung-back thin streak of blood where her lip had been torn on the right side.

It was dark before they got back. When they rode into the wagon circle people came from all directions. They stood in dumb silence as the riders swung off, placed the bloody blanket and its burden on the ground, let others lead the animals away and stood like *sopilotes*, still as statues until Betts turned where several clucking women were leading her away and said, "Do something for him. Paw, don't just stand there!"

Men abruptly moved, talk commenced, the silence which was now broken became filled with questions.

Calvin and the lanky man watched as Rick and his blanket were carried to Martha Oakly's wagon. The old woman was beside herself, giving orders, gesturing, fluttering as she warned the men lifting Rick into her wagon not to drop him. They had to grunt and hump and squeeze amid the wagons crates, bits of furniture, tinned supplies, before they came to the thick bedding back near the tailgate. They eased Rick down there, trooped back out and as they reached the ground each emigrant gave the old woman an unpleasant scowl. They were in the company of enough flighty, scolding women particularly in their own wagons, to look tolerantly on the snapping and faunching of someone they considered mentally one brick shy of a load.

The camp had guards out all night, in relays, although no one thought the Good Lord would be unkind enough to send them another unpleasant visitation, for a while anyway.

Two wagons showed lamplight through their canvas covers. One, at the northerly end of the camp on the east side, echoed muted sounds of female gabble. Three women in there were helping Betts Calhoun bathe, salve her injuries, and eventually to allow her to lie down on some floorboard blankets and sleep.

The other lighted wagon was on the opposite side of the circle not far from the Oakly wagon. In there, three men and a boy were sitting like old buck Indians, solemn as owls, passing a bottle around, bypassing the youth, in fact acting as though he was not among them, making growly statements and grunting questions.

The lanky emigrant with the Adam's apple had examined the corpse while lashing it behind his saddle. He shook his head gently in rebuttal to something Mike Calhoun had just said, "Maybe you're right, Mister Calhoun, only when I straightened him out before lifting him over the back of m'horse, I saw something interesting. I knelt down and looked close . . . It couldn't have been Mister Telly who shot the son of a bitch."

Calhoun turned his bearded face. "Why?"

"Well sir, near as I can figure it, Aaron was looking for Mister Telly where he was wedged between them

250

two rocks where we found him. Calvin picked up Mister Telly's gun. It ain't been fired, so I'd guess Aaron saw him an' shot him . . . Now then, the bullet that killed Aaron come from behind him . . . The slug didn't make the kind of hole a Colt'd make."

Mike Calhoun's forbiddingly darkly bearded face did not turn from the lanky man. He said nothing. The lanky man smiled a little. Because he had a cud in one cheek the smile looked lopsided.

Calvin Stuart swallowed once and bypassed Pat Calhoun to hand the bottle along. As he did this he said, "Mister Calhoun, I expect you knew Betts's been carryin' a derringer for some time."

The large man's head turned slowly. "Yes, I knew that . . . Betts? Are you sayin' Betts shot Aaron?"

Neither of the other men nodded nor spoke, they simply sat there looking directly at the large man, giving stare for stare.

Calhoun looked at his son. "Pat, go over yonder where they took Betts an' see if she had a gun. If she did, bring it back."

As the youth departed Calhoun swallowed once, passed the bottle to the lanky emigrant and finally showed expression, although it was difficult to see, what with the light being poor and his face covered with beard.

He smiled. Both other men also smiled. The bottle made another round then was tucked under some bedding. By the time Pat returned and climbed inside, the older men were sitting in tired silence. Pat hunched past his father and dropped a derringer at the older man's feet.

Mike lifted it, broke it open, smelled the barrel from both ends and tossed the gun over to Calvin Stuart. When the lanky man had also made a satisfactory examination, he leaned to pass the little weapon back to Mike Calhoun as he dryly said, "Folks hold them little belly-guns in contempt. A preacher of the cloth once told me Mister Derringer had sold his soul to the devil, who set him to makin' hide-out weapons . . . Now that can't be true can it? The devil wouldn't make a gun to kill his own kind, would he?"

Calvin replied. "Ask Reverend Spencer."

The lanky man softly snorted. "When the fight was goin' on I passed his wagon. He had two guns on pegs. He was down on his knees prayin' so hard he didn't hear me rattle the tailgate." The lanky man paused. "The shootin' an' killin' kept right on. Gents, I'm more likely to believe it warn't the devil who set Mister Derringer to makin' them little guns." He smiled at Calhoun. "I expect Betts might agree with me."

The whiskey, plus being able to relax after so many hours of hardship and tension, caused the meeting to break up. None of the three palaverers were young men; hadn't been young men in a hell of a while.

As Calvin and the lanky man climbed out of the Calhoun wagon their attention was drawn to feeble light showing through patched canvas on a wagon northward. The lanky man tapped Calvin's shoulder as he said, "'Night, Mister Stuart." He walked away leaving Calvin gazing at what had to be candle light.

He was tired enough to sleep on nails, but something made him forego his bed. He walked over to the feebly-lighted wagon, noisily climbed from the wheel hub to the deck below the driver's seat and leaned to pull aside the canvas.

His greeting was vituperative. "A man your age sneakin' into a widow-woman's wagon in the middle of the night! In the mornin' I'll let folks know what you done. I'll have you know I'm a respectable — ."

"How is Mister Telly, Martha?"

The tirade abruptly stopped. The old woman looked around where Rick was lying near a candle set in its own wax atop a dented cooking pan. Without returning her attention to Calvin she muttered, "You could have waited until morning. How was I to know you'd come sneakin' in here to see him?"

Calvin hunched forward until he could see Rick. It was on the tip of his tongue to tell the old woman, that in all his seventy-four years, he'd never snuck up on a woman, but if he had now, in his late years, decided to do that, it wouldn't be on a female whose damned wagon was so hard to climb up into.

He hunkered studying the younger man. Rick's wound was scabbed over. In the feeble light he looked like a warmed over corpse, but his chest rose and fell with an even cadence. He looked filthy, unshaved, his face was swollen. His lips were chapped, his shirt had been removed. His stomach had scratches as though he'd been clawed by a catamount.

The old woman broke past Calvin's observations. "I got water down him.

He liked to drunk hisself to death if I'd of let him. I got some badger broth down him too. He sort of drifts in an' out. He rambled for a spell, only it didn't make no sense an' part of the time I couldn't make out the words. I think he was praying. Several times he said a name — Gabriel."

Calvin hunkered in long silence, then arose, lightly tapped the old woman on the shoulder and hunched his way out of the wagon, climbed down, smelled a chill in the air and headed for his own wagon.

At the time he'd joined the Calhoun train he had told himself in all seriousness that a man in his seventies had to be insane to cross a continent seeking a new life when the one he had was just about done with. He also told himself as he tooled his wagon into place among other wagons, that when a man thinks of age instead of horizons, he's already more'n two-thirds dead.

Rick did not become aware of the world and his surroundings until his second day in the Oakly wagon. It was another day and a half before he felt strong enough to climb out and bat his eyes to keep them from watering in the full glare of a sunbright afternoon.

Martha had done what she could with his attire. It was in poor shape but she had scrubbed it. His face gave the impression of someone having been yanked through a knothole. But he felt better, his strength was returning rapidly; if someone had told him what kind of broth had hastened his recovery he would not have gone near Martha Oakly again as long as he lived.

The third morning as he climbed out of the Oakly wagon to hunt up someone who owned a razor, he met Betts Calhoun. Except for her face where Aaron Copeland had struck her, she was presentable, clearly clean, freshly attired, her hair had been taken care of.

They stood looking at each other for a solemn, silent moment, then she said, "Do I look as bad as you do?" and smiled. He grinned back. "No, you look pretty as a yellow bird. I know what I look like. You wouldn't have a razor, would you?"

She turned, beckoning for him to follow. She had two straight razors, both in boxed cases. Each razor had ivory handles and a whetstone. While he was honing the blades she brought a small table from the Calhoun wagon, a towel, and a cake of homemade brown lye soap. For a mirror, which she held for him, she had a highly polished square of steel.

Lye soap got folks clean but it did not lather, which made shaving with the stuff rather like setting up each hair to be pulled off the face rather than shaved off.

He shaved without flinching; what the hell, life was a series of inconveniences, he was fortunate shaving was his only current one.

She didn't laugh when he winced but her eyes twinkled. When the shaving was finished he washed, ran damp fingers through his too-long hair and grinned at her.

She had been thinking of something else and did not grin back. "I expect you know Aaron is dead."

He seemed to have heard that sometime during his half delirium. "I remember a shot that knocked some piled rocks apart. I remember raising up to see where he was . . . That's all I can recollect."

She spoke soberly without smiling. "He piled those stones, then snuck around to be on the far side when he shot into them. I think he knew about where you were but he needed movement to be sure . . . There were two more shots, Rick. The reason you don't remember them was because his second shot was at you. It missed by about six or eight inches, struck the big rock in front of you, a chunk flew off the rock and hit you square in the face . . . I thought you were dead, there was blood all over. I thought he'd shot you in the head. I came over — ."

"What about the third shot?"

She put the steel reflector atop the table before answering. "I crept around until I saw him watching you . . . I was about fifty feet back when I shot him."

He stared. "You had a gun?"

"The derringer I kept inside my dress after he dragged me off a horse one time. I would have shot him sooner, but the others were around, or he kept me in front where he could watch me. He told me if I moved he'd cut my throat. That was when he went lookin' for you. I snuck after him, didn't get a good straight shot until he raised up to shoot you."

Betts's father called from around the wagon. She called back. Big Mike Calhoun climbed over the wagon tongue and stopped. He looked from his daughter with the bruised face to the man with her who had the appearance of someone who had been through a meat grinder. He said, "You make quite a pair." He was referring to their injuries but they seemed to think he meant something else. Betts spoke crisply. "If you'd turned up into the rock field instead of riding on by, we'd look normal enough."

Calhoun overlooked that and smiled at them as he addressed his daughter. "Your little gun's in the dresser drawer inside the wagon."

She remained annoyed. "You're going to say I shouldn't have shot him in the back."

"Betts, anyway you could have killed him was the thing to do, even if he'd been asleep." Calhoun allowed a moment to pass before speaking again. "Mister Telly, Calvin's got your four big horses tied outside the wagons. If there ain't one broke to ride we'll tie one out there you can ride."

Calhoun considered the basin of dark water, the razor and steel mirror on the table for a moment. "We're hitchin' up. I reckon we can make that town down yonder you mentioned with the livestock we got. Down there I expect they'll have horses for sale." Calhoun raised his eyes to Rick. "We owe you a lot. Folks would like to pass the hat before you ride home."

Rick gently wagged his head. "They don't owe me anything, Mister Calhoun. I came for my horses, the rest of it just plain happened. I'm obliged for getting my horses back, I know folks paid Copeland for them."

Calhoun leaned on a fore-wheel. "They'd like to have a special supper this evenin' before you ride out."

Rick was uncomfortable. "That's decent of them, only I'll just ride one and lead the other three horses back home."

Calhoun lingered as though he had more to say, but in the end he shook Rick's hand with a powerful grip and went back to where the other emigrants were striking camp.

When Rick faced Betts she was regarding him very soberly, and that added to his discomfort. He held out a hand which she took, and squeezed hard, then released it.

"Somethin' I'd like to ask you, Betts."

"All right."

"I know you're goin' to Oregon, an' I know you got your paw an' brother to look after — ."

"Pat's big enough to take care of himself, and Paw never needed looking after."

"Well; it's quite a ride back to my ranch . . . I'd better get started."

"Rick?"

"Yes'm."

"Tell me about your ranch."

"There's not much to tell. I've been building it up. In a few years it'll be big enough so's I'll need a hired man. It's good country, real pretty. My home is a log house with four rooms. I finished a barn two years ago, Gabriel an' I put up a nice set of holding corrals . . . Betts?"

"I don't know, Rick."

"You got roots. You got family."

"I don't think that's it . . . Are we

talking about the same thing?"

He made a crooked little grin and held her gaze with his eyes. "I think we are."

She leaned to re-arrange the items on the small table. "Can I have more time? I . . . have strong feelings for you; I just need time." She looked up quickly. He was gently smiling at her.

"All the time you need, Betts. I'll be at the ranch. Without Gabriel I'll be busy as a kitten in a box of shavings." He moved slowly toward her. She turned just as slowly. They met in a strong embrace before he turned to depart.

As he rode one big horse with three others trailing, she leaned in afternoon shade watching. She did not move until he was out of sight.

★ ★ ★

It was a hard winter, Rick moved his cattle as often as was necessary where there was shelter and feed which they had to paw through snow to reach.

The big horses recovered, by spring they had regained all their shrink. They, unlike the man who owned them, remembered nothing of their ordeal the summer before.

He worked hard, slept like a log, arose ahead of sunrise and continued to work hard. It was after spring had passed summer was abroad when he rode into his yard one late afternoon and saw the buggy with its dozing seal brown mare at the tie-rack. He dismounted to lead his horse into the barn and stopped dead.

Betts smiled at him. She was a picture of health, and had her hair fixed just right. She said, "You've lost weight."

He did not see Calvin until he went toward her. The older man was standing half in shadows inside the barn. He nodded without speaking. To Calvin, who had volunteered to come back down here with her, this was *the* moment.

Calvin had lived a long time, he was not by nature a gambler. They had come one hell of a distance, had been on the trail close to a month, and right now, within the next few minutes, he would know whether it had been in vain or not. He leaned, watched the younger man, watched the handsome woman, and prayed hard for the first time in thirty years.

Rick looped the reins of his saddle animal, walked over and opened his arms as he said, "Betts, if I live to a hunnert this will always be the greatest moment . . . There's a preacher in Crested Butte."

She laughed as she went toward him. "I worried you might already be married."

"Naw," he said, holding her close. He winked over his shoulder at Calvin, who turned away; seemed like for no damned reason when a man got older every now and then dust or something made a man's eyes water.